Molly Path

Molly Path

Eugene O'Toole

Molly Path

Text copyright©2022 Eugene O'Toole

Cover©2022 Nikki Daigneault

ISBN 978-1-8380247-9-6

3 5 4 2 1

First Published in Great Britain
Hawkwood Books 2022

Printed and bound in Great Britain by CPI Group (UK) Ltd.
Croydon CR0 4YY

For Margaret.
A good teacher can change a life.

I

1

The front door is ajar. I notice this after I have realised the bell does not work. It cannot be right.

My fingers hover over the frosted glass and I feel its ridges, but I do not push. I look down at the mattress bent double on the grubby verge outside the house then upwards to determine its trajectory. It was thrown from the window.

It is soaked and filthy, trampled underfoot, and I can tell it has been there for some time. The house is darkly ominous even though it is morning. I am concerned.

I push with one finger at the door and it opens to a small hallway with stairs ascending in front of me. The carpet is threadbare. Flecks of matter, dust or dried food, have been pushed to the sides by the action of feet. It smells like an old hessian sack.

I lean inside and call out.

Hello? Anybody home?

Nothing.

I'm not sure what to do. Bernadette said it was going to be a hard case.

'One last nut to crack before you go, Eileen.'

But I have never been in this situation. All the experience in the world does not prepare you for this.

I can feel myself hoping the girl is safe. It is pressing upon my shoulders, the need to find and protect her, to lift her out of this squalor. And I have not even met her yet.

I take in the other terraced houses, tiny identical boxes repeated ad nauseam throughout the estate. I want to see signs of life, seek reassurance, but there is no one there. I am alone.

'The family is troubled, Eileen.'

I step inside and repeat my call so that if I encounter anyone they will know I come in peace. I'm not an intruder. I whisper what I'm going to say under my breath so I am prepared.

I'm a tutor from the education authority. I'm here to see

Molly.

But the only thing I can sense in this house is my voluminous apprehension. It is inflating to fill the space. I want to know where the child is, to look her over, make sure she is seen.

*

I'm the moron with piss for perfume, and he points at me with a snotted finger.

His anger loops, and they turn in their seats. I'm surrounded by eyes peering from within sickly red rims, clogged with the hardened yellow gunk of sleep. They're stacked in endless columns and rows like tins of beans in Tesco Metro. They're all staring at me like I done something wrong, as usual.

My eyelids flicker, and my chest slides against the cotton sheet. My heart pumps with fretful friction. The mattress is warm. Wet.

Mr Butler stands to attention at the front of the class handing back homework, his face etched with anger. I panic. School has this effect.

The huge stone walls of Calton High rise from a wasteland like a castle. Its windows are made of black glass, the roof is held up by tree trunk beams, the hall is the size of a car park. On the concrete floor, pupils sit at desks under the watchful eyes of a scowl, Butler, eternally maddened, his chest stretched taut.

A tight band of pain slices across my ribs. A bread knife saws through my flesh. Blood oozes from a wound. I put my hand to my throat. I hear laughing. I open an eye.

*

I am intending to climb the stairs, but I need to find an adult first. I must ensure everything is in order. I poke my head into the kitchen off the hallway but it is dark and empty, so I stand at the bottom of the staircase and look up.

The stairs are narrow and steep and the carpet is coming away. I put my foot on the first step.

Are you up there?

The silence is stubborn and aggressive. I'm tempted to call Bernadette to ask for advice, but she is depending on me.

'She won't come out of her bedroom. You're the only one who can do this, Eileen. Please.'

I hesitate, and wonder if I have created a rod for my own back. What was I thinking? Was I trying to put off the inevitable?

*

I stare at a gap in the curtains from the bed. They're starched, sad, matted dust grafted to fabric by years of gloomy light. They're a wall bricking up a window, or might as well be. Once red, they've faded through to a pattern of swirling pear drops like seahorses. Or tears.

Pays-lee. I saw that design in the *Bella 2007 Christmas Special* I found on the bus, although I can't remember the spelling. As I lie here in bed, I'm gripped by a need to find it.

I trace the outline of a seahorse with a finger in front of my eye, then close it. Such relief. But I'm left wondering what it'd be like to have a seahorse as a pet. I could keep it in the bath.

I've left a gap in the curtains to look out. The estate spills across a rutted expanse strewn with litter and littered with cars. I never alter that gap, not by a millimetre. It's my world. Don't want to twitch the curtains in case anyone looking in sees them moving. Twice a day, I squint out. Once when I heave my skinny body from my bed, usually in the morning, and once before I collapse back into it, which could be any time at all.

But there ain't no point watching what goes on out there, because nothing goes on. The overcast sky seems always fit to burst with rain, an unchanging shade of dreary grey same as concrete. A rusting *Fee-at Pan-der* ain't never moved. It squats, in a strop, a sullen waste of space, blue once. Moss grows in soil on the windscreen. A white Ford transit van coughs like my mother when it wakes the neighbourhood at the crack of dawn every other day. Sometimes when I look out it has gone, leaving an empty space, but then when I check later, it's back. It belongs there, waiting in boredom for its owner, heavy on its haunches like a bulldog. Faded writing on its side. Something to do with windows.

One day, I will drag myself out of bed to look through the gap and note that the jumbo crisp selection packet has finally gone. It's been pasted since my childhood to the greasy tarmac, pinned to the ground by the *Fee-at Pan-der*'s rear wheel. Inert trash.

Time stands still. At least today is transit day, and it woke me. I went back to sleep. This don't bother me, because it gives me a kind of routine in the empty space what is my life. Reminds me, don't it, when it's the other day and that there's been a day in between even though I ain't noticed. It is as if, by waking me, it gives me the nod to sleep again. Because I'm exhausted. I've blown a fuse.

I'd still be sleeping if that woman hadn't disturbed me. At first I listened. Then I dozed off again.

In the third space beside the other vehicles sits a yellow *Honn-der Si-vv-ik*. It's new, only been there a while, and a welcome sight. The paint still shines enough to lighten up the place, so I know it can't possibly stay. Everything new on this estate soon disappears. That car has a kind of grin and slanted lights. A funny face. I like it.

I kind of remember cars when they're named after animals. Most come from China. A *si-vv-ik* is a Chinese squirrel and *pan-ders* live in China as well, in a place called *Fee-at*.

Not exactly sure where China is. Far away, that's all I know. And I don't remember lots of words.

*

I begin to climb the stairs. I call again, but there is no reply. At the top, the atmosphere is stale. The landing carpet is dirtier than in the hallway. I can see scraps of tissue, cotton, a curler, hair woven into the fibres.

There are three rooms. The door of the bathroom is open and I hear water dripping, but the other doors are closed. I guess that Molly's room is smaller than her mother's and so beside the bathroom above the kitchen. I look at the door. It is painted ply, once smooth and white, a blank canvas, but now smeared with years of scuffed dirt. There is a hole at knee height where it has been kicked.

I rap on the door with my knuckle. I can feel it is thin and light. It is full of air, there is nothing to it, but the girl behind it is as trapped as any prisoner.

Molly, are you in there?

Nothing.

I put my ear to the door to listen. It is as cold as the rest of the house and I wonder whether the heating is working.

I rap again and try the handle just once, noisily, so that she will know I'm here.

Nothing. I'm concerned. I have visions of a teenage girl harming herself, cutting her arms, attempting suicide. Now I want to shove the door with my shoulder and barge my way in to check on her, but I know that even though it's flimsy, I'm not strong enough. I'm too old.

Are you going to open up?

I listen again. All I need to hear is a sound of movement so I know she is all right. Just one sound will suffice, then I can rest easy.

Nothing.

*

I'm Molly Path and I'm an empty space in a car park. Can't do nothing. Stella says so, and she knows all about being useless.

I live in a house with a broken TV. I live in a house with a broken washing machine. I live in a house with a broken boiler. Sometimes I live in a house with broken lights. I live in a house that reeks of brandy. I live in a house with Stella but not with Stan.

Can't spell nor do maths nor sport, can't remember nothing, can't make friends, don't have no pen. Am ugly as sin and the others said I stink of piss.

Deserve everything I get, don't I? Don't deserve no friends. Deserve to be mocked. Never look good, do I? Never put no effort in. Why bother?

Am in the wrong body?

Get a fright in the mirror when I peel away the cornflakes packet. Greasy hair the colour of rinsed mud without kinks or curves, straight as straw. It screeches beneath a brush like a violin. Don't even grow from my scalp, but oozes then congeals in a fringe like lava. Can't never pin that fringe to one side nor shape it. Just returns. Like vengeance.

Could have drawn it with a marker pen, a line across my gormless forehead, but I saved that for the unibrow. Thick eyebrows merge above my nose. '*Planet of the Apes*', Bianca said. Once wore a pair of sticky glasses I found on the bus. Gave me a headache. She threw them out the window.

Collect spots like stamps and my nose arrives half an hour before my face. A gherkin on a plate between pickled cheeks. A mug served up at a fish and chip shop. Zombie lips, so grey I must be dead. My mouth turns down. I smile in reverse.

Skin like a sandwich bag containing toothpaste. I am a negative version of Stella. Her tan is like the paint job on the *Honn-der Si-vv-ik*. It lasts a fortnight. She does something in the bathroom with cream. Once she clogged the toilet with her tissues. Stank the house out. I had to unblock it. It gulped like the tramp outside Tesco Metro.

So what's the point of school?

Can't teach me nothing don't already know. About being useless. About being ugly. About cruelty, *pays-lee,* parked cars, litter. About broken houses with blocked toilets. About tanned arms that never hug me.

*

I look across the landing at the other bedroom. It is possible that I have picked the wrong room, but I'm already pushing my luck. Then that door opens. A washed-out blonde stands there, sleepy, wrapped in a dressing gown, curlers in her hair, bewildered. She is unsteady on her feet and looks at me strangely, her eyes straining to focus. It is as if she were drunk. A waft of stale alcohol in her perspiration reaches me and I realise. She is drunk.

What's all the racket?

She slams the door shut.

I'm disconcerted. She is drunk. It is 10 o'clock in the morning. But I am also relieved. At least she is here.

I knock at Molly's door one last time. Something has clearly disturbed her, because now I hear movement, a bed creaking.

I won't stay out here. I'm going downstairs.

*

I'm tired of being tired. It's time to dream about being dead.

This is something I do every day in bed at about the same time, but I think I live outside time and don't know whether it's morning or evening no more. Could be dead already.

Being dead ain't very different to being alive. Probably better. This time, I decide to look down at my dead body from above. Perhaps it's rotting, but I don't do smells very well because there are so many of them in this house I can't tell the difference no more.

Anyway, I'm looking down at my dead self, and this particular dead self looks quite good if I say so myself. She's laid out in the kitchen on the table like an ancient goddess. My body wears the princess-style pink tulle wedding dress what Jordan wore when she married Peter Andre. I recognise it, so puffy it almost fills the kitchen. Someone's done my hair and it's wavy, with ringlets at the temples. Thank God they sorted out my fringe.

A flower has been placed behind my dead self's ear because apparently someone *cares*. My unibrow has been plucked and I'm wearing eyeliner with a hint of gold. Whoever slapped on the foundation did a proper job, because there ain't no molehills. My dead self is smiling, her lips upturned, her smile the right way round.

I am pleasantly surprised. I should die more often.

I search the crowd to see if anyone is crying, because I want to know if they are sad that I've croaked, and who put the flower there. But no one blubbers. They're chatting instead, like it were someone's birthday.

The woman who keeps knocking on my door is there, although I've never seen her face to face, so I imagine her as a skinny, frisky type who don't use make up but wears an anorak. She's as plain as rice, but even so my mother's boy squeeze is ogling her arse and I can tell Stella is getting shirty, because she's pushing out her boobs above the hooped mini skirt she nicked from Primark to show off her tan.

There's a tasty spread in the front room. Stella couldn't possibly have made it because she can't cook a bleedin egg, so that will have to remain a mystery. People are milling about eating fancy snacks containing slimy mushroom paste. No one cares about the hairs in the carpet, thick as a rug, or the bloodstains on the battered sofa that Stan lifted from a skip. Mr Butler's there, but only for the grub. He's dribbled mushroom paste on his shirt, messy git. They stuff their food like a bunch of pigs. Vol au vents fall and are trampled into the hairs.

Bianca suddenly turns up. The queen of Calton High. She is half wearing a micro-skirt and all legs, her hem so high it is above her head. Although I can't budge because I'm dead, I feel a growing sense of panic.

What's this? The whole class tramps in after her. The court of Queen Bianca squeezes into the kitchen to inspect my body. I can see their eyes, millions of them, guzzling me with judgment.

A rubbish tipper turns up outside. It's my hearse, and there's Stan, gormless as ever. He hops off the back, his sleeves rolled up, and enters.

The walls bend inwards and press down upon my dead self on the table. The colour of my dress changes from pink to dirty brown, my unibrow grows back, my ringlets fall out, my make-up soaks into my skin, my zits come back.

Stan lifts me like a sack of sand. The others watch him heave my dead self up and sling me over his shoulder. They file out to form an honour guard, and now the whole estate is there. He carries me solemnly, but no one weeps. Then he tosses me into the dumper. Trash.

Everybody laughs. But that's not the worst of it.

The worst of it is that they *know*.

2

They met in a lane leading to a tattered farm under the battered chrome of an empty Kentish sky. He was raking asphalt and she was looking for a man. He was tongue tied. She felt the gravel beside the culvert pressing through her soles.

Stan did not know her name. He had never seen her. But he recognised her all the same. He knew where she had come from. It was not her gait or how she dressed, the deprivation of her underfed body lean in a feral way because it had never been domesticated, the pink tracksuit with white stripes grubby at the cuffs, the flaunted hoops. It was instinct.

He pointed down the lane to the junction. It was the best he could do. She could not resist him.

Stella examined the shaven hair on his neck, burned lobster red above the line of white where the skin folded softly over the collar, his burly forearms frothing with small curls extending from rolled sleeves, the missing button on his chest.

She was looking for the gaffer because he would pay her to do things his wife knew nothing about. It was an easy way for her to survive and she did not hate the man or the fact that he stank of sticky blacktop and sweat. To feel his fat, sunburnt, calloused palms pressing upon her young body, to be lifted by the small of her back effortlessly like she were a feather, to be the weight that is lifted, were sensations she did not deplore.

Stan did not say a word. Nor would he have done so were he to have understood. He stared awhile, then pointed down the lane to a shabby caravan in a layby crowded with road rollers. Everything he meant to say was in his eyes. As she kicked up dust, they told her. He was what she had been looking for.

It was unnerving, the penetrating reach of his gaze. He knew everything he needed to know, without comprehension. He knew she was not lost, but willingly adrift, because she understood that is what it meant to live and anything else would be to tame something wild.

They walked away together. They were good at that.

When he finally spoke, trying so painfully to inquire who this was, she could barely interpret his garbled cant. He wanted to know what it was they shared. Although questions did not form easily in his mind, this matter weighed heavily upon it with ancestral mass. He was rarely given to inquiry of any kind, preferring to be the answer and not the query, but on this occasion he could not help himself. After that, he did not bother to speak. Stella spoke for them.

This magnetism never resembled love, but loyalty, with its charged vectors of prejudice and passion. Although they did not communicate, they spoke a language of sorts because the assumptions they made coincided. They occupied a caravan and managed, but Stan would never fully know what his eyes had seen. He would never fully know her.

When he began to drift farther away to lay driveways and car parks, Stella did as well. She travelled alone again but in a bottle seeking the gaffer or others like him to fill the space Stan left.

That was it, two itinerants pulling in different directions without a destination. They had always been adrift, but they drifted farther apart because they had never been tethered.

When they found themselves in a house on a bleak estate that stood stubbornly still and was built for lost souls, it was too late. It could have had wheels because although it was fixed, it was neither a home nor an anchor. But it did not move at all.

Then somewhere on that confused journey Molly joined them, and was unnoticed.

3

This was no ceili 'social'. This was music from across both seas.

Jive and rock 'n' roll rushed like a flood into a rural vacuum to wash away the farmyard muck. Who could have imagined? In Knocknasnaa.

Eileen had showband fever.

She was in love with Brendan Bowyer, as was every girl for twenty miles, for that is how far they would come to see the Royal Showband. In Kerry. In the parochial hall. Imagine.

She was imagining, a little too much. Her face was turned to the window but did not see the fields. Mr O'Connor was not happy.

Eileen Murtagh, could the river-field ever be as verdant as Yeats?

She snapped out of her reverie, rigidly erect and penitential. Nonetheless, she would prefer to be reading *To Kill A Mockingbird.*

She tried to recite with the rest of them.

'He wishes for the Cloths of Heaven ...'

But all she heard was Brendan's voice.

'Come down the mountain Katie Daly.'

Mr O'Connor looked at her. She knew her Yeats inside out. She was too clever by half.

Does anyone have any questions?

She had a question. But it was not something the fencepost of a teacher with stapled eyes could answer.

What should she wear?

She would have to raise her game in the glamour stakes. Brendan would spot her from the stage then turn up on the doorstep of the farm clutching wild roses and fuchsias gathered from the lanes beside the river. She would escape her mother at last.

She could not possibly go to the concert in the pleated grey skirt and blouse that she wore to Mass on Sunday. She might as well wear a potato sack.

She had bought material and made her own dress on Aoife's kitchen table, the pair conspiring over a cut-out pattern. Aoife's sister Deidre was giving her a loan of her ankle strap sandals. Deidre had her hair done at the hairdresser's in Listowel and Aoife had slept with rollers. All the girls looked different that Friday. They were all going to the concert.

Even though Eileen's mother had forbidden it.

*

She wiped the rain from the saddle of her bicycle and dried it with her mackintosh.

A green clump of moss had washed out of the drainpipe descending from the gutter of the schoolhouse and sat directly under the front wheel. She edged it away with her foot, then wheeled the bicycle down the muddy path.

Aoife was waiting on the lane. It rose gently between the fields, hedgerows giving way to stone walls. At the top, they hopped on to their bicycles and coasted down a mile, then pedalled furiously at a lonely green post box. Aoife accelerated ahead. Eileen shouted after her.

Remind me to buy some momentum next time I'm in Reilly's.

Cows chewed in the lower pasture. The air between the fields was fresh. The slope flattened then wove through a copse where sometimes they climbed trees to peer at the fledglings. In spring they had spied a blackbird's nest in a forked branch.

At the crossroads, they hopped off to survey the gradual descent to the white speck of a dairy before the River Feale. On a clear day they could trace a faint outline of the Mullaghareirk Mountains. Cycling that lane became a daily race to see who reached the dairy first, but there were no odds on the outcome. Aoife sped past.

They hugged the bank of the swollen river flowing

doggedly towards the sea, taking it carefully, mindful of a neighbour who veered in and was swept downstream, saved only by an overhanging blackthorn.

The river flicked suddenly to the south, taking its menace with it. The girls coasted on the flat until Aoife scraped to a halt at a roadside shrine.

Nine o'clock, don't be late mind!

Eileen watched her disappear, then turned into the fields and wheeled her bicycle along a scraped rut to the shrunken plot.

When her father died, her broke and bitter mother had sold off their fields one by one. All that was left was the pasture surrounding the cottage and the right to use the track. A landlocked country.

Eileen jumped from her bicycle and allowed it to clatter against the cottage. Carved scars in the plaster would be all that was left of her when she was gone. The wheel gradually lost its spin until, at last, it stopped.

What use were her mother's prayers? When Eileen left, all the prayers in the world would never bring her back.

*

It is a prayer that she will need now. Eileen will have to pray for invisibility when she climbs out of the window.

Her mother's iron refusal still chimes. When the woman forbade her to go to the concert, she was sitting at the scratched oak table with all the tension of a tightened strap, her straw white hair dangling, blocking her eyes. Her mouth was turned down like an upturned saucer. She was waiting for the slightest movement to reel in the line.

'Prostitutes dance like that. It is the Devil's work.'

Father Hanlon does not think it is the Devil's work, Eileen reminds herself as she now sits in silence alone at the bare table after school. The good father organised the whole thing. Everyone for miles will be going. He needs the money for the church roof.

'*Why does she fuss over the open hearth like a hen dressed in black? Every other woman in Duagh has a range. It has been so for ten years now. Why do we wait a holy eternity for the food to cook in skillets hanging from a crane over turf? The unseasoned wood she scavenges burns with sparks. They will ignite the thatch. Why does she dispatch me to the spring with an enamel bucket? Why does she insist on reading her precious Lives of the Saints by paraffin lamp?*'

Her mother enjoys the strain. She needs the pain.

Aoife persuaded her parents to let her go to the concert. They were easily persuaded. Eileen's mother barked at the Moon.

But the girl has a plan. She has been preparing for weeks and gathers her thoughts, goes over it again. Every Friday, at this time, she has declared she is awful tired after such a week. She has so many chores in the morning she will go to bed early to get her rest.

So she pours herself a glass of milk, cuts two slices of bread and stuffs them in her pocket, then makes for the lopsided staircase.

Is that you?

Her mother now lurks in the other room. Exasperated at the cheek of her daughter for coming home at all. Not even a gasp of a greeting. Eileen smiles. Her plan is falling into place.

I'm real tired, I am, I'll go to bed early, ma. I can be up at the crack of dawn to start my chores.

Is that a faint laugh she hears?

Up with you then. You'll not be wanting supper.

Eileen grins like a cat and closes the bedroom door noisily for good measure.

4

I doze. Not surprisingly, in my dreams I find myself in my room, but this time there are two beds in it like there used to be. Before my mother set the other one on fire.

Stella is snoring like a road drill. She's been celebrating on the brandy, because she's got a new bottle of brandy. It is the kind of deep sleep that a hibernating Chinese *pan-der* has in winter, so deep it don't wake up even if you set fire to its mattress with a fag.

I replay what happened. Dirty black smoke suddenly fills the room. Flames appear from inside a hole in the bed that yawns like a mouth. The choking plastic smell of burning foam.

I remind myself in my dream that I have to wake Stella before she burns to death. She splays across the mattress with her dribbling head and clumpy legs dangling over the sides. When she's roused, she curses in slurs, as if chanting mysterious poetry. Her tongue slaps the air and leaves it smarting like it's been spanked for giving her lip.

It's only by good fortune that she's blocked the toilet in the bathroom with tissues smothered in tanning cream. I had put a pan beneath the pipe to capture dripping, foul water, because it was leaking through the floor into the kitchen downstairs. I drag the pan to the bedroom and throw it on the flames.

Amid a buzzing beehive of slurred curses, Stella rolls down the stairs to the stained sofa.

But now in my dream it is the morning after, and there's no poetry, slurred or otherwise. Just Stella telling me to,

'Clean up the bleedin mess.'

She throws the mattress out the window.

Stella ain't a morning person. She rasps like a seal for fishes until she's had a fag. A battalion of phlegm has assembled on her tonsils preparing for a full-scale attack on her throat. The daily Siege of Stella's Gullet. Throttling her from inside. Strangled by mucus.

Eventually she warms up, then rattles like a chainsaw, hacking chunks from old logs like greying men with pony tails at country fairs. That voice can fell trees. It chops off limbs and tosses them into the path of passing transit vans driven by bald double-glazing fitters. They don't have a prayer.

As I lie in bed watching these images skip playfully in front of me, I try to smother her face with a pillow. It's my way of taking control. It's the least she deserves.

Pain helps in these situations. So I kick violently with my heel, thumping the wall beside my bed. I recognise the dull thud of plaster giving in. The acid sting offers a distraction, and I reach down to rub my foot. My fingertips stick together with the warm glue of blood.

I feed on that pain. It's my breakfast, because there ain't none to be had downstairs. It breaks through the confusion to remind me that I'm not a figment of my own imagination. I've still got a body. I still feel things. In a strange way, pain gives me comfort.

Someone knocks at the door. There's the low roll of a voice outside, as if a wind is blowing.

It's not Stella. It's that woman from the education place. Wasting her time.

I reply in my mind.

'I'm sleeping.'

*

There it is, that voice again, the gentle waves of an accent like sea on a beach. It isn't muffled by the breezeblock like all the other howls within this house. It's more like butter melting into hot toast. It soaks in, rousing me softly from my dreamy state.

Both my eyes are open now, although they don't seem at first to be working proper and everything is a blur. I rub my face and feel dribbles on my chin.

'I'm so tired.'

The fact that the woman from the education thingy is still

turning up rattles me. She don't seem to get the message. But deep down I know resisting would be pointless anyway. I'd never even whisper it, but truth is I *want* to go to school. I'm tired of being at home. I'm tired of being alone.

I picture the girl I thought could be my friend at Calton High.

I'm sitting beside her, and we're about to do a spelling test. Mr Butler circles above the class like a peckish vulture looking for scraps. She sees that I've got nothing to write with. She rummages in her pencil case, brings out a biro, hands it to me.

'Go on.'

She jabs it. A banana for the monkey.

I ask myself again, as I have a hundred times, why didn't I take it? I froze.

No one has ever lent me a pen before. It raised troubling questions. Did it mean that I could keep it for other lessons? What if I forgot to give it back and the girl I thought could be my friend then called me a thief? Did I have to replace the ink when I was finished? How do you refill a biro anyway? Where do you get the ink? What if I'd broken it as I fumbled through the day? I'm useless.

So I shake my head. She raises her eyes, and Mr Butler is so angry he actually glows when I hand in a blank again. He speaks loud enough for the whole class to hear, because he wants them to.

'Why didn't you borrow a pen?'

I stand there studying the strange oval shape of some chewing gum on the floor. The girl I thought could be my friend raises her eyes even higher than before. They almost hit the ceiling.

She was special. Above her pretty brown eyes fluttered the longest eyelashes I've ever seen. I wanted nothing more than to touch them with my fingertips, to see them bend under gentle pressure, to sense the needle-like feeling of tiny spikes.

Her hair was dyed jet black and she cut it in a bob. It swayed like a skirt when she spoke. The other girls copied Bianca, swinging a pony tail low at the side, but she did not.

She'd escaped the queen's almighty power and was saying something else.

'I'm different.'

I pull the sheet from my face and wonder what the girl I thought could be my friend was doing at that moment in school. I wonder where she lives and what her bedroom looks like.

Most of all, I wonder what would have happened if I'd taken the pen.

5

We walk the trail. The Slieve Mish Mountains are as imposing as grandparents and wear their woodland against the mist like ancient shawls. We pass through a grove of beech and cross the bridge spanning the meandering Owencashla.

Eager trees compete for our attention as we stroll the serene valley rising to Lough Carun at Glanteenassig. Spruce and lodgepole pine, silver fir, alder and holly. The air is still and the silence real, all sound swallowed by the rising hills.

It has been a long journey.

We picnic at the lake and idle in the clean air until the light begins to fade, then return at dusk to Aoife's warm house in Tralee, the mountains merging with the distant night.

She is happy in her home, grounded with books and silken links to a family scattered in the peat but still living here and there, a smattering of nieces now with children of their own.

The farms at Duagh are ruins long gone, but not the memories of them and we know that this is the time and place to share them sitting in the darkness at her fire, allowing night to wrap around us. There is magic here and I feel it.

Aoife knows that I will join her. I have travelled many roads but I shall return soon. I see the house that I will buy, identical to hers. I see my fireplace flickering, the brooding peaks through the kitchen window, the life to come. I am reconciled.

I know I am alone, my inheritance in the soil, but my father reminds me that he is with me still. He cups my face with the basin of his ploughing hand.

'It is all right, child.'

He whispers, his laboured breathing an echo in the night.

'Do not fret, my special girl.'

I stand beside his grave, bidding him farewell. He rests, his hands crossed upon his farmer's suit, his kindly smile eternal.

But my mother does not rest and that is not a smile upon her face. She lies beside him somewhere but would kneel and pray some more if she could, her endless confession unfinished. You cannot confess after death.

She sat there in the kitchen as he slipped away, a cold vigil as austere as every moment of their union, her hands clasped like twisted wire, but not in prayer that night. She should have called the priest, but something held her back. She sent me.

Her rancour became the furniture of our lives, a bitter home to leave behind. I became her penance, and when I left it was for good. I left that life to start another. We would never speak again.

I hear the ringing of a bell and I stir. It is a clock. It is morning.

I realise that I am no longer there, in Ireland, and although the relief is colossal I know now that only dreams can show us where we have been and where we are going.

*

I wake. I blink. I remember. I am in London. I have not been in Ireland for what seems like a lifetime.

I extend my arm and switch off the clock, half asleep. I notice the liver spots on the top of my hand and the wrinkled skin hanging beneath my forearm but do not recognise them. They must belong to someone else. I close my eyes again to order my mind.

It is a new day, and I feel that fountain of optimism that powers me like a battery. I cannot help it, it charges by itself with the rising of the sun. Thus it has ever been. It is less vigorous, of course, its force drained by insecurity, but it is still there after all these years.

I push the covers aside and swing out of bed. The stiffness in my back reminds me that there was a time I rose with the vitality of a sprite. I rushed to help my father in the fields.

As I drive to the Mudlark centre slowly through the grudging rush-hour, I replay my conversations with Bernadette.

I think I am trying to convince myself I have done the right thing. It was flattering, being asked to come back so soon after retiring. And that feeling of excitement had returned as I looked through the thick manila folder, piecing together the broken fragments of Molly Path.

But this child is buried deep. It will take time to dig her out. I fear time is running out.

I had been planning to start work on my house, painting and cleaning over the autumn to ready it for a sale. Spring is the best time to sell, and in between now and then there will be a lot to do. Retirement has been postponed.

I find myself going over my finances in the traffic. I have enough money, a pension now, and do not have to work. But moving back to Ireland will be expensive, and what I earn from this extra year will come in handy.

I reach the gates of the centre and pull into the car park. As I walk towards the entrance I look through the windows. I see my former colleagues gathering in the staff room, the same old faces, superheroes achieving the impossible.

It is going to be hard putting all this behind me.

*

I study the kitchen door in Molly Path's house, but think of another door long ago.

Oak panels dabbed crudely with the thick gloss paint left over from the eaves. Droplets had formed at the base before it had dried. One had splashed to the cold floorboards, a solid spot of white forever fused to dark wood. I sat on my bed examining that door from the inside, the sturdy cross-beams, the hook for my towel, the old handle that clanked with a metallic twist when it turned, the fathomless keyhole. I can remember my father painting it, filling the frame with his bulk.

I shake this thought from my mind, and stare at the kitchen in Roundwell. Making a cup of tea here is like searching for dry firewood in a wet forest. But in the silence my mind again drifts back to that door in our cottage in Duagh. Locked in my bedroom, I had stared at it for a weekend, my mother's footsteps recriminating on the stairs. Doors are symbols.

I stir my black tea. I have managed to dredge a cup from the foothills of a slag heap in the sink of filthy dishes, foil containers and pans without causing a landslide. Somehow, I was able to wash it, even though there was no headroom to steer it beneath the tap and no washing liquid. There was no tea in the cupboard, either, but I have brought my own. A trick of the trade.

*

Molly is my swansong.

I told you it would be difficult. Refuseniks always are.

Bernadette told me so, I admit. But it is little consolation to be reminded of this as I sit in her bright office discussing what to do next. I have taught children who refuse to go to school before, yet this is a different kettle of fish.

You could always lie in wait on the landing. Ambush her. She has to leave her room sometime. To go to the toilet, for a start.

I'm not in the business of sitting on the landings of unfamiliar houses. I remind her that I am officially retired but doing one last freelance job before I pack this in for good, and I am only doing it because she begged me.

I did that, Eileen. And you know very well why. You have the patience of Job.

This may be so, and I have been told that I have a well of patience so deep that were you to fall down it you would never escape. However, time is no longer on my side. Right now I could be sorting out the contents of my attic, packing up, and arranging the sale of my house. I could be house-hunting in Ireland. I could be planning the future that I have decided to embrace at last after so many years away.

Yet I know what Bernadette knows.

She knows that I will yield. It is an instinct as deep as the roots of the ancient oak tree that dominates the lawn outside her window.

I watch this skilful, persuasive woman and marvel at how she lures me into her web, pulls me to her cause with such traction. There is mischief etched on her plump, round face, but that grin does not mock, it smiles knowingly at the innocent ambition she sees within, the compulsive vocation, the yearning to mould something from nothing. A passing fool might dismiss this rotund orb of nervous energy as a cook or a cleaner as they search the corridors of the Mudlark special education centre for its manager, but if we have both learned one thing in the twenty years we have worked together it is that appearances are always deceptive. Bernadette understands a simple truth. That there is art in what we do. And that I still yearn to create a masterpiece.

Take as long as you need.

But I do not want this to endure. I fear that if it takes too long I shall be diverted, change my plans. Yet it is clear from the scale of this problem that I am in it for the long haul. The rest of the school year at least. Ireland will have to wait.

It is either the surfeit of optimism that has carried me through my life and is the characteristic I most admire in myself, or weakness, but as Bernadette speaks I am already trying to imagine what I can make of this child. And delaying my move will give me the time I know I need. There is much to do in my house before I can sell it anyway, many pieces of the puzzle to fit into place. Above all, the next home I buy will be my last. Bernadette is giving me the time to choose well, and Tralee is not going anywhere.

Can she actually read my mind? She senses strongly that I will rise to the challenge. Out of loyalty to her. How did she inspire such allegiance?

We conclude by agreeing to hold weekly meetings. She says she intends to be '*hands on*'. If only this child knew what forces we muster, what unstoppable momentum we generate. Bernadette has done it again. It is a marvel to behold.

I decide to do what I have done so many times with the

troubled children taken under the Mudlark's wing.
Wait and see.

6

Molly sighs. She is awake again, and the woken world is worse than that of her dreams. It is easier to sleep.

By now there is a dent in the plaster beside her bed because she has been kicking it for weeks. She suspects that if she keeps kicking the wall in the same place, she will end up next door.

She imagines herself bursting through on the other side like a miner completing a tunnel. Mrs Nally sits in bed in her curlers, sipping a cup of tea. She is surprised to see Molly, but offers her breakfast anyway.

'Shreddies? Or dog food? I hear you prefer it ...'

Molly reflects on Mrs Nally with some regret. Her elderly neighbour goes shopping. That is all she does. Her record is stuck. But at least she does something.

The only time Molly ever sees the old woman is when she waddles up the pavement with a carrier bag carrying lumps. She takes that path every day, come rain or shine. The lumps must be tins of dog food because the poor dog barks his head off in the hall and only stops when she reappears like a daily miracle. A miraculous old woman who disappears with an empty bag then reappears with food.

Molly knows that if she were to force herself out of bed right now, step out of her room, go downstairs, and walk out the front door in her underwear with her bleeding heel, Mrs Nally would be there. Returning from the shops with her lumps. The old woman would not even look up but would fix her tired old eyes firmly on the weeds in the cracks as she walks straight past and puts her key in the door then coughs as she enters. The dog would bark with sheer relief at this magical reincarnation, then shut up again until tomorrow.

It is a mystery, Mrs Nally's bag. It is never full and never empty. What's more, she does not even need it because she has those sagging udders that old women have which pull their necks towards the ground with such baggy weight their spines arch and contemptible boys on estates like Roundwell shout,

'That's a funny place to hang your shopping bag.'

Mrs Nally could use her udder bag to carry her lumps.

But Molly understands. She senses that Mrs Nally just needs a reason to go out. Molly also wants a reason to go out. To go to school. She *wants* to go to school. Just not that school.

And there was a time when Mrs Nally spoke. She said hello. Smiled.

Molly does not remember exactly when her neighbour stopped talking, but she does remember why: Stella.

Her mother was with a bloke who was not Stan and they were necking. At least it looked that way to Molly from the upstairs window, pink tongues flicking like lizards amid a blur of her bleached hair and hooped earrings and his shiny baldness. She could smell the spearmint. They may have been trying to eat each other, because they were going at it so hungrily it was as if they were starving. Molly knows what it is like to be hungry.

Molly did not know this man, but he could have been anyone because he shaved his head and so did every bloke on Roundwell. In fact, he was everyone.

From upstairs, his smooth head glinted like an egg without a face. That was what the estate was. An egg box. They were not free range and mostly going off. Quite often they broke. Sometimes they broke each other. It was hard to make anything interesting with them. They were just fit for scrambling.

Stella and the egg were making a meal of it.

Then Mrs Nally came home with her lumps. She did not say a word. It was enough.

'What you staring at?'

That was all it took to silence the old woman.

Stella cut out her tongue with a saw-toothed knife then nailed it to her front door as a warning.

*

The shame of it. Molly will ache forever from a wound so deep it cuts to the shrivelled kernel of pride that remains somewhere in her damaged heart.

She still feels the nakedness of her bottom against her coarse woollen skirt, still feels their eyes on her back in class. They knew that beneath that skirt was nothing but her stinking backside. Bianca told them.

The changing rooms reeked of piss and detergent. Bianca took her clothes and tossed them into the locked cubicle. Molly should have left her knickers there. She should not have crawled under the door to retrieve them from the bowl and put them in her pocket. The odour from the floor stuck to her like sweat.

This recurrent nightmare halfway between sleeping and waking exhausts her. She needs to stay awake for it to go away. And she is tired of being tired.

She listens carefully.

Even from beneath the sheets she hears shuffling outside her door. She hears that woman stomping up the stairs, the landing creaking beneath her feet.

I can't teach you like this, can I?

There it is again, the voice. How many times has it been? How long is she going to keep coming? She knows Molly will have to leave her room. She knows she will have to go to the toilet. She is waiting outside to pounce.

Molly wishes she would stop knocking. It sounds like the echo at school, the hollow slap of the woman's hand bouncing from the door. She pushes her head beneath the pillow.

The woman is going down again, her fingers squeaking against the bannister. She is stepping over the bunched carpet where it is coming away from the stairs. She is careful.

The drumbeat fades. Molly hears a chair scraping in the kitchen.

Is her mother home? Is she splayed across the lopsided mattress, paralytic, hugging her empty bottle like the child that Molly is no longer, so incapable of waking she could herself be dead? Molly will not see her for the rest of the day, or possibly even until tomorrow. She is relieved.

She has never seen the woman from the education place. She has only heard her voice, and so it is hard to imagine what she looks like. Can a voice create a face? She wants to see her.

The woman wants to help. And Molly wants to be helped. It is school that she hates. The people. They know what happened between Stella and Stan. They tell her so in nightmares.

There are footsteps on the stairs again, then another rap at the door.

I'm waiting, Molly. I'm not going to teach you through the door. Come down when you're ready. I've got all day.

It is old, that voice. It is not the voice of a skinny woman in an anorak as plain as rice. It knows how to get what it wants. It is a teacher's voice. It is returning to the kitchen. It is doing what it said. What should she do?

*

Molly stirs and pulls the sheet over her head then pins it with her fingers beneath the pillow. A sickly film of drying sweat, oil from her hair and dribbled saliva has soaked into the foam in the outline of a head. It has her odour and she rubs her face into it for reassurance. Her nose bends then springs back into shape.

Stella's nose had bent like that. It came out of nowhere. A swinging bare-knuckle left hook at the bottom of the stairs so fast it created a gentle rush of air as it hurtled towards her face.

But Stella's nose had not sprung back into shape. It had remained flat, as if the bridge had been ironed but someone had forgotten to do the nostrils.

In Molly's mind the story of that flattened nose had passed into legend. And Bianca knew exactly what happened, as if she had somehow been watching everything.

She must have told the others who told Mr Butler who told all the teachers who then told their classes who went home and told their parents who told the people at work who told their friends.

The whole bleedin country knew about Stella and Stan. And when they saw Molly in the street or on the bus, in the playground or in the changing room, they knew she was their daughter. Molly could feel their eyes peeling her raw.

In bed, she recounts this legend every day, a vernacular Greek tragedy set on the circular stage of Roundwell.

A detective would have deduced the story from the spots of blood flicked in a crescent along the hallway wall. Another reminder of the short-circuit that has drained the battery of that home. Just stick your fist into a socket.

The bloodstains on the wall are brown now, so ingrained that even vodka would not get them out. But if blood is what you're after, then there is also plenty in the sofa, because when Stan stuck his plug fist into Stella's socket she staggered to the front room to sleep it off and dribbled generously into the cushion like a blood donor.

The next morning, for once in her life, Stella had been quiet. Either she had forgotten what had happened, or had thought better of vomiting it up again like a curry gone off in the fridge.

But then again, it was not Stella who had seen Stan just after it happened, jerking a dusty suitcase from the wardrobe, tossing it on the bed, pulling out drawers, filling it carelessly, stomping out as night blanketed the estate. It was Molly.

She had watched him from her bedroom across the landing under the yellow light of a flickering forty watt bulb as he flung in holed socks, shoes, a sweatshirt, struggled with clasps, and issued a low, incoherent growl similar to that of a disgruntled *pan-der*. Even his suitcase was half empty.

With an impending sense that this departure was different to the rest, Molly had desperately, urgently, oppressively, wanted to communicate with her father, to hear the sound of his reply, to forgive him simply by listening to his incoherent efforts to justify himself because she had begun to realise he was not to blame for who he was, even though she was to blame for who she was.

But she did not.

Instead, perched on the corner of her bed with throbbing

anticipation, she realised she did not know who Stan was other than a man who laid asphalt driveways, occasionally emptied bins, and on the rare occasions that he spoke, did so in an accent no one could place.

She was frozen in an obvious conclusion, mesmerised by self-hypnosis, understanding right then that if he went out the door he would probably never come back. Then she would never find out who he was, why his left eye drooped and he had a blurred tattoo of a donkey on his forearm, why he ate raw onions and apple cores. Molly would never learn the meaning of the strange words he uttered with such difficulty or why Stella taunted him like a cat.

She would never know why he was her father.

His footsteps pounded on the stairs, a drumroll before an execution. She yearned for them to stop, shuffle back up. But the front door slammed and the house shook with the finality of it all. Only Molly felt this, because her mother was out cold on the sofa donating blood.

Stan was gone.

7

S tan found a caravan in Whitstable, slouched beneath a metallic sky so wide his mindless gaze could lose itself in wandering. The clouds stood still for him, a foreboding shroud, and he recognised the air with its smell of cobbled shingle, hints of carbamide and turning oysters.

It was a four-berth tourer with a fibreglass lantern roof and a little fridge that had seen better days, and it would do. To Stan it was a mossy palace.

The site manager was round and, apparently, happy. He boomed breezily of fish and holiday seasons from within a Hawaiian shirt beneath the salty air, and twirled a white moustache dating from the Raj. He understood these folk, so let Stan have it for a steal. He knew him from before, and he was good for it.

There was a job laying tarmac at a stables, just built with shiplap cladding, and the gaffer sensed that Stan was around, for Stan was everyman. It set him up for winter, and he liked to watch the animals as they stared back at him with a humble confusion that he was familiar with. A memory stirred from childhood. There was once a donkey.

It was a Sunday and there was nothing to be done. The ether was heavy with torpor, and he sat at the table in the caravan and watched the drizzle beading on the windows. It took him back to a place that seemed much the same, lazy long afternoons stretched out listening to his da, ma, brothers, always listening.

It did not matter that he could not remember when or where this was, because in a place mostly concealed he knew where he was from and who he was. This place was always Stella and always Stan. Simple really. He gave no thought to it, although he had little to give.

*

It gnaws, inside. He does not understand what is happening and wants to stop and scratch at it, tear away the skin, find out where this feeling comes from.

He brings the rake down hard upon the unyielding mound of tarmac and strains to pull it into position, so hard the muscles in his shoulders nearly tear. He feels the pain, but that is the point.

Stan misses Molly.

He breaks lumps of sticky gravel with difficulty and spreads them as evenly as he can, the muscles in his back screaming with the effort as he stands motionless amid acrid fumes like a demon in a simple kind of hell. But he is no longer aware of the pungent smell. A callous on his palm has cracked and caustic vapour bites it, the discomfort so real his hand shrieks. But even so Stan does not stop. Pain is no distraction.

No matter how hard he tries to change the subject, he continues to see Molly, and when he relents and allows this thought to push all the others to one side something in his stomach still gnaws. He cannot rid himself of the idea that he will never see her again.

A memory comes as he sits in the caravan alone at night, staring into space. It is of Molly and she does not speak but sits with the dog in the doorway of a caravan in Sheerness. Stella berates her. That voice circles and caws like a seagull. His brain clenches his fist, tighter. Stella cackles, tells him he is pointless. Not a real man. Like the latest fellow passing through that terminus of bleached hair and painted nails.

Molly is watching him struggle to understand. She is sitting on the step when she sees a bottle spin towards him in slow motion. It misses and explodes against the door, but slices her arm, scares the dog. The mongrel scarpers across the campsite, back legs to shoulders. Stan leaves. It would not be the last time.

Next time he sees Molly he is on the bins in Roundwell. He looks up at the window as he lugs a green plastic wheelie to the dumper, and she is there, looking back at him from within that cold house without light in a fixed place where people stand still until they die, and even stand still when they are dying.

Stan feels something. It takes him time to figure out what it is. Yes, he feels sorry for her. Alone with Stella. It is an unusual sentiment for a man with few thoughts.

Then, suddenly, he finds himself back here, in Whitstable.

It is hard for Stan to order his mind. He is powerless, a leaf blown helplessly in a gale. His feelings are a well of confusion. He inhabits a perplexing, complex world where the easy words others use prick like thorns in hedges around fields containing battered caravans.

Stella only ever makes it worse.

8

Molly barely slept for weeping. Her whole body strained with the violence of her sobs. A torrent of unexpected tears soaked into her pillow as if she were pushing her face into one of the giant puddles that formed in the car park behind her house and swallowed up entire families.

Her chest heaved so much she could hear the muscles ripping. She buckled under the full weight of woe that she had accumulated in her short life but had been saved drip by drip in a piggybank of pity for that moment.

Molly lay in bed, catatonic.

The next morning she knew Stella was in pain, because for once the woman shut up. Her mother's pain resided in her broken nose and eye sockets bruised black, a temporary setback comparable to the gas being cut off. It did not reside in her heart. And so to kill her pain, Stella went straight back to the brandy before breakfast even became an option.

Without a thought for her daughter, she bathed like Cleopatra in a bathtub of booze until she ran out of cash again. The dwindling Paths had the most musical bin bags in Roundwell, bottles that played a symphony of chinks to delight jaded neighbours with bemused dogs.

Molly was despatched to nick sunglasses from Boots. She swiped a pair when the serious Indian woman at the counter turned her back.

For once in her life, Stella was happy. For ten seconds. From amid an alcoholic haze, she saw herself in Sharm el-Sheikh wearing Jordan's Oakley crystal pink shades. And she would give absolutely anything to have Jordan's boobs. Stan would not have decked her with that flick of his tarry hand if she had Jordan's boobs, she mumbled to no one in particular as she sat in the kitchen trying on her new goggles.

But then the seal flapped and the chainsaw buzzed and

EUGENE O'TOOLE

Stella let out a mean, throaty rasp sharpened to a razor by far too many fags. It was so raw it bled. The sunglasses were ... too ... small.

'Useless cow. Can't even nick the right bleedin size.'

Molly stops dozing as she replays this memory.

She pushes her fingernail into her wounded heel, and the rush jolts her with narcotic intensity. She brings her hand to her mouth and tastes her own blood. The iron bitterness is real and raw. This is her life. The pain reminds her that she is not outside looking in. And it reminds her that everyone else is watching. They had seen Stan deck Stella in glorious Technicolor. They had seen him pack and leave. They had watched her weep, and gloated.

They knew what Molly was. The worthless child of worthless people, a dog's dinner who wore no knickers with piss for perfume.

9

Stella likes boys. She liked this boy. Her father would have put his foot down when she stayed out because it was their way. He would have. But the boy was Big Bob's son.

They ran away and huddled in a bus shelter and he touched her where she knew he shouldn't. They came back because they had no money and her mother knew what they had been doing. She hit Stella with the back of her hand and split her lip.

Her father was of a mind to pay Big Bob a visit, but it was all for show. No one questioned Big Bob's boys, especially a man whose daughter was a cocky slag.

'Fockin ... wait till I ...'

Another empty threat, the kind muttered over pints of porter in the company of weaklings who can smell lies because they live by them. Either way, the boy could take her father easily. He was already a fighting man.

So Stella's withering father bit his tongue and was quick to do so, put up and shut up, and her mother never let him forget. The girl learned from that. She listened to her mother's admonitions. She watched her father take it like a cuckold. After that the threat left in him was not even idle. It was empty. He shrank into something else entirely, a receptacle for whiskey until Big Bob had had enough and threw them off the site.

They wandered the lanes without protection or direction. They had no destination other than a desire to keep moving, prey to any policeman or petty bureaucrat who chose to make their lives a misery.

Stella's mother blamed her husband, but blamed her daughter more, because she was already used to doing so. She had already blamed her for breaking that family. She had already abandoned her dreams of a big wedding and a dress made in Birmingham paid in cash. All the woman dreamed of now was making ends meet.

A social worker showed up. Stella had been caught shoplifting.

'She's no child of mine,' her mother said.

Then when Stella burned the caravan with a cigarette, it was the final straw. The reckless girl would have to go.

10

Stella is in the kitchen sucking juice from an orange, although in this case it is a cigarette. Nonetheless, she draws on it with a slurp, then gulps the breath down into her lungs forcibly like a reluctant hostage. On a good day she can finish almost an entire fag with one, long, unbroken inhalation. A crooked digit of ash dangles precariously, ready to fall with the slightest judder. It is as if the cigarette has become her accusing finger.

Her bleached hair flops across her face and half covers it, but she does not make an effort to push it away from her sunken eyes. These languish deep in their sockets with a weariness that is hard to fathom. Around them are bagged cushions of skin smeared with yesterday's eyeliner. Those eyes are as tired of her as she is of herself, and when she mocks the people around her which is often they roll with an autonomy that could be mistaken easily for madness. Perhaps it is.

Pinhead pupils scan through the mesh of her hair, hiding in the shadows like a cat watching unwitting prey from behind the foliage. They follow Eileen as she enters the kitchen, but the head does not move, Stella's atlas and axis fused as an assertion, this rigidity sending a message of inflexibility. Her sagging night-dress patterned with faded red roses has seen better days.

Eileen stretches her lips in a curt, non-committal way. It is her business smile, a trifling courtesy to smooth rough edges when meeting someone unpleasant. She places her satchel on the small table and pulls out a chair. She examines Stella surreptitiously, able to read danger at once. An atmosphere of hostile intent clinging to an odour of evaporating alcohol.

When Stella finally pushes her hair away, she speaks as if she has been doing so for weeks without a rest, a hoarse depth of tone that is inescapable. It is the cigarettes speaking. Her voice is pure nicotine, its pitch billowing smoke.

Bleedin useless, she is. Won't come out.

She jabs at Eileen to make the point and the worm of ash waiting its turn to escape her flicks itself from her cigarette to the table top, free at last.

*

Do you mind if I make myself a cup of tea?

Stella gestures at the kitchen and laughs.

Help yourself.

It has not changed since Eileen first started coming. The mountain of dishes in the sink is the same avalanche about to happen. They still block the light, but Stella's gesture indicates that this is nothing to do with her. She believes this. The kitchen has come to represent a geological feature of the limited landscape that she inhabits. The unwashed dishes have calcified into rocks. She gives no thought to when this petrification occurred, because time seems to discontinue around her, waiting to see what she does next. She has jettisoned all chronological baggage in order to stay afloat. The only time that matters is the time that Stella creates for herself.

Ain't no tea, though.

She laughs again, but this is more of a challenge, full-throated mockery with the weighty punch of a leaden cosh.

Eileen is prepared. It is a skill she learned in the volatile presence of her own mother. She smiles and opens her handbag, then pulls out a teabag.

I have my own.

Stella is wrong-footed, just for an instant. Eileen notices her head wobble, almost imperceptibly, thrown off balance. She is strangely disappointed. Her forehead furrows and she tries to conceal herself behind her cigarette, which is not easy.

Eileen watches as Stella gulps again and feels the vacuum this creates in the kitchen. She half fears this dishevelled woman will suck the air from the house and they will both suffocate there in front of a sink piled with dirty dishes.

40

Waste of your time ... what's your name again?
Eileen.

Stella pulls again, but the cigarette has given up the ghost. She has smoked it to death.

You Scottish?

Once her hair has been pushed away, however, Stella reveals a symmetry framed by high cheekbones that remains attractive, even softened by the wrinkles forming around her eyes and mouth. Her eyelashes are naturally long. Her lips are finely fashioned. She still relies upon her face to be an invitation.

The bridge of her nose, however, is unmistakably flattened. Eileen has seen this before.

Sound a bit like my Stan.
Stan?

Stella pauses, scanning Eileen's face carefully. She senses she is being interrogated, but cannot deduce how. She jabs her cigarette in the air above her head to signal a location that could be anywhere.

Her dad. Bleedin bastard.

It is bait and Eileen says nothing, but listens for clues, learning from every word and inflection. She expects a monologue and folds her hands patiently.

Bleedin useless he was, too.

The cigarette is already dead, but Stella stubs it out anyway then reaches for the packet to discover it empty. Fallen ash is smeared along her forearm and she does not rub it away. Eileen notices the long, black smudge on the inner side of her arm, beneath which is a pink scar sliced across the egg white skin. This is licked by fake orange tan that has dried like cheap gravy. The colour runs across her wrist like a sleeve then over the top of her hand to the sickly dark nicotine stains on her claws.

Stella tosses the cigarette packet across the table. It falls to the floor.

Don't have a smoke do you?

Eileen shakes her head. She gives nothing away. This

woman's predatory manner necessitates caution. The smell of a prowling animal poses imminent danger.

Stella merely huffs, dissatisfied, a mistress of the unpredictable. She eases herself out from behind the table and makes for the door, her slippers flapping on the clammy vinyl. She stops, but does not turn round.

How long you 'ere for?

Eileen turns and speaks to her back.

As long as it takes.

Stella nods, trying to suggest that she has knowledge of a deep secret. She is sucked through the door as if she were now the smoke drawn in by the huge dirty orifice that is her home.

*

It is another day of waiting, but the kitchen sink has become visible to Stella at last, because she sees in it an opportunity to absolve herself.

Look at that. Been like that for weeks. Lazy cow.

Stella is in the habit of weaving tension around her like a cat's cradle and half expects the mound of dishes in the sink to tumble when she stabs her cigarette at them.

But today this dark magic will not work. Eileen deduces that Stella is growing frustrated at her persistence and, to disarm her, pulls papers from her satchel. She places them in a pile on the table and flicks through.

Stella watches her like a tiger, checking her fingernails in between tugs, distrustful eyes trying to peel back the older woman's skin.

Eileen goes for broke. She couches her question in a way that cannot possibly be misinterpreted because it places the onus of responsibility solely on Molly. She has deduced that Stella does not take responsibility for anything.

Has she always been like this?

Stella bridles, loses her cocksure sneer. To her mind, this has to be a trick question because it seeks to measure how much she knows about her daughter and, therefore, how much she is to blame. She hesitates, fumbling for coherence.

Yeah.

The strain of responding is etched into her face. When questions have sprouted in the past, she has been in the habit of stamping on them. Keep the thickets down.

Useless cow since she was born.

She turns matters to herself. Safer territory.

I had a caesarean you know. Left a bleedin scar that long. Want to see it?

To Eileen's surprise, Stella yanks up her T-shirt.

Molly is just a scar to her.

11

There's no lead in my pencil. I'm unable to sketch a face from the air that fills my head. My mind refuses to visualise.

The education woman is out there. I can hear her footsteps shuffle up the stairs, then slide back down. I can hear her voice, burbling tones that float like bubbles. I like it, even though I don't want to.

I press my head back and stare at the blank ceiling, as wide awake as I'm ever likely to be. I've been imprisoned beneath that grey sheet for weeks, bored to death. To bleedin death.

I try to force an image but it's hard. Cooperate, I plead with my own head, but my mind seems to rebel at any effort. The woman is waiting in the kitchen at the table or in the front room on the sofa right now, but all I can see are a table and a sofa.

She sounds tall, if that's possible. Her voice is muffled by my door but arcs down from above, like a ghostly hand reaching out to touch me. She's old, because it's kind of deep and not afraid of secrets. It's confident, it doesn't hesitate. But it's not washed out and she ain't ancient like Mrs Nally. It still has an edge to it.

I'm surprised to discover that if I open my eyelids slightly, my vision blurs and it's easier to focus. I want her to have silver hair as a sign of age, but in neat pinned plaits as a sign of youth. Hesitantly, I squint and squeeze out an image of a teacher, although this one is short and her hair is black. Then she turns and points her crooked finger, a hag, and I close my eyes because she's a teacher at my school and I ain't never going back there.

I decide the woman downstairs is different, she doesn't snap, has no sting. Let's be honest, who'd do her job? Come to a tip like this in Roundwell to wait for someone like me to come out of the bedroom? It's even more boring than lying in bed.

I feel weight upon my chest and wonder if it's hunger, but I know it's not because I would recognise that. Hunger is the opposite, it is anti-weight, a hole you need to fill, and I am feeling something else. I owe this woman something. She came for me.

I slip my legs from under the covers using just that thing what makes everything fall, you know, *grabity*. It's effortless and my feet float slowly to the floor. It requires no energy and I could be on the Moon. But now I push myself up and feel my muscles stretch and crack. In a mirror I see a smudge of skinny body. It's wearing underwear. Its heel is black with bruises.

I search for something to wear and find a jumper in a pile of stinking clothes. I sniff the armpits. They're rank, but I pull it on all the same.

My face looks at me with surprise. It ain't spoken to no one except Stella for weeks and needs to practise. It might have forgotten how to talk.

My lips curl and and my tongue twists as I mouth what I want to say. I repeat this several times, although there ain't no sound. Then I remember I've got to force out air from my chest to make this work.

Slowly, it comes, soft at first, imperceptible, but then stronger like opening a bottle of Fanta too quickly, exhaling, until finally I hear myself as she will when I leave this room.

No one ever comes for me.

*

I hesitate. I peer down the staircase, a mountain climber who has lost her nerve. It is steeper than before.

I study my bare feet and bend my toes to grip the carpet. The nails are dirty and I know this ain't good. I've forgotten when I last washed. It's not a priority.

For several minutes I stand there, swaying trance-like on a cliff. I like the feeling of being on the edge, but also knowing I will not fall. I strain to listen and there's movement in the kitchen, the clink of a spoon in a cup, a vibration through the weedy skin of this terraced house. I know it ain't Stella. She slurs, sleeps, sits and smokes, but that's all she ever does.

The sounds stop, and I'm worried. The woman will jump out and catch me frozen there, no longer in my bedroom. I can still turn back. She'll be none the wiser. But when I see my bedroom door, I don't want to go back in.

Another noise. A cough, perhaps, and I know there's a living, breathing person in this house who is not my mother or her latest bloke. The very thought of it makes me nervous.

I trace the scuff marks and dirt on the bedroom door, imagine the bed inside. I realise that I'm standing in light flooding in from a different window, and cannot go back. The boredom is too much. It's crushing.

I study my hands, and can feel that light. It strokes my skin like a feather. It feels good. I turn back to the stairs, and thoughts come to me as I sway, not knowing whether to plunge down or sit and wait. An epic struggle rages, a war of possibilities.

It's a trap.

The woman with the voice will raise her eyes with something vicious in mind. As she shambles about in the kitchen clinking cups with spoons she plots, waiting for her moment. Then the cruelty will begin again. This time I'll have no escape.

No. It's a rescue.

The woman with the voice will release me, break the spell. She has soft tones and she is waiting. She's come a long way to see Molly Path.

*

I'm at the threshold. I smell the damp clawing from beneath the soiled lino on the kitchen floor. It smells like mud and the pattern is of paving stones. I position my toes right at the line where it meets the blackened carpet in the hall. Dirty toes on a dirty threshold between dirty linoleum and a dirty carpet in a dirty house.

When I'm alone and Stella is in her room, I go into the kitchen to feast on cereal. The surface sticks to my feet, peels away with every step, as if a layer of skin is being stripped. I anticipate the sucking sound and the sensation on my soles.

But now the woman from the education place is in there.

I hear a spoon clinking again. I don't know where she found the tea, but she's made herself a cup all the same.

She must be sitting, because there's no sound of peeling feet and so I ask myself which side of the table she is sitting at. Stella's side looking out, or my side looking in?

If she's sitting on Stella's side she'll be a tourist. She'll marvel at Bowl Mountain rising from the Valley of the Sink. When I was little I had no toys, so I played with the dirty dishes. I stacked those chipped bowls and cracked plates up like a mountain, then ran the tap water down them in waterfalls. The rotting peas was trees. The takeaway tubs was the shacks of the mountain people. Stella didn't care because she thought I was washing them.

This stinking mound don't bother me no more, although I'm sure it'll bother the woman from the education place. Bet she's fussy about things like that. But I know I'll have to wash them one day soon because Stella will start throwing them at me if I don't.

If the tourist sits on my side of the table, she can visit the art gallery. The multi-coloured stains splashed against the wall by the swing bin are like graffiti, but really old, as old as what the Romans wrote on one of them buildings they had with pillars. And every colour has a different flavour. Ketchup. Curry. Jam. A kind of mosaic of stains.

Once again I try to imagine what the woman looks like. Tall and thin, I decide, tight and serious. Her silvery grey hair is tugged and pinned. But still the face I want to see does not appear. I have turned this into a game, gambling against myself that she will be as I imagine. If I'm right, I win a prize, even though I've got nothing to give myself.

She doesn't know I'm here. I crept down as silently as a cat.

I could be a hunter if I wanted. I sway on my toes and dig them in, teasing myself, feeling the barrier between the lino and the carpet, enjoying the sensation.

Will I go in?

I know now I will not go back. I'm tired of being alone and this woman has come to see me.

I step forward.

12

Stan drifted through days like pollen, travelling in every sense. Nothing remained the same across the hours, his eyes fed without the morsels of landmarks, faces always fleeting blurs lacking features. The only ground he stood on was himself and it was not rock but shifting sand. Stan flowed. His instincts remained loyal but out of reach.

He himself had an inkling of this when he looked in a mirror, and could become lost for long minutes, drawn magnetically back towards sensations he could never quite remember, eyes clouded with elemental residue.

Stella stopped him doing that. The trance annoyed her, so Stan no longer stared in mirrors but stole glances at them as if they were preparing to steal something from him. He shaved as quickly as he could so as not to be lured through the glass.

But there was an absence. Stan was the expected guest who never turned up. His mother called him *'difficult'*, *'hard to fathom'*, ceaselessly bemoaning as a curse a disability she had no words to explain. His father just despaired. The boy was not like the others, he was confused, he could do nothing right. There existed an insurmountable barrier to communication. No matter how hard he tried, Stan could not make progress. They were exhausted.

Stan knew something was wrong, but never what it was. He tried to piece together clues, to nourish this notion with titbits of evidence. These were adduced by his meagre memory at random moments when he least expected, sudden bursts of loud noise in an otherwise quiet night that disturbed his waking dreams.

It was not that he was bad, in the sense that there was cruelty in him, because he knew he was not. When he looked at a donkey, a geyser of sincere emotion overflowed uncontrollably and he wanted to put his arms around its neck and feel its hirsute warmth against his burnished skin. His mother brought him up under the sign of a cross and Stan knew who the Devil was, even if his da did not.

Stella was of little help because she did not understand him either and did not have the patience to try. There was only one reason she was with him and it was neither love nor dialogue. They recognised something in each other they had once known, and what they recognised was themselves. It made sense to be together, even though it made no sense at all.

Stella was a question without an answer. The worst thing about being with her was not understanding what she wanted. Because Stan wanted to give her what she wanted.

It was too late now.

That, at least, he understood as he watched the spray slipping down the window of the caravan in Whitstable.

This reminded him of Molly, because it took him back to a rare memory. Another caravan, on the Isle of Sheppey, where the girl had played with a stray all week and he had gone off to lay asphalt and Stella had been worse than usual.

It was the first time the family he had tried to create had travelled away from the home they lived in without wheels nowhere near the sea. As that home in Roundwell did not move, neither did they, in mind nor body. This was evident in their mood. Static, fixed, reflected inwards.

In that home, Stan, Stella and Molly were waiting for something that never came. Possibly a future.

13

As Eileen drinks her tea, something attracts her attention, a hint of air on her cheek, an equilibrium disturbed. She strains to listen. A door scrapes against a carpet with the brushing sound of water, a floorboard creaks.

She crosses her hands and fixes her eyes on the entrance to the kitchen. The weight of the footsteps coming down the stairs is not the same as before. It is not Stella.

Eileen adopts her firm but fair face, the one that says *'I shall not harm you, but I have a job to do.'*

The movement stops in the hallway, outside the kitchen door. It hesitates. Eileen understands what it means to step across a threshold.

Molly enters.

*

This girl could be pretty, pleasant to look at if a little plain. Her cheeks are well-defined, a little too sunken for comfort, but her eyes twinkle, even if they do not enquire. She has a few spots, but nothing that could not be sorted out with concealer. Her hair is untamed, but could be easily threatened with a brush. She is only wearing a jumper above her underwear. Is there method in her madness?

Eileen sees a blush radiating across the girl's face.

Molly, is it?

She extends her hand but the child does not appear to know she is meant to shake it. Molly sits down and stares at the table.

Have you had your breakfast?

Molly is rigid.

Eileen has already looked in the fridge for milk, but it is empty. She stands and opens a cupboard. There is a box of corn flakes and she puts it on the table.

There's no milk. Do you want a bowl?

Molly shakes her head. She pushes her hand into the cereal packet and withdraws the last fistful of flakes, the powder of the remnants sprinkling the table. She begins to peck at them one by one, like a pigeon, and when the pile in her hand has gone down, she begins to nibble what is left slowly.

Eileen watches her in silence and smiles. She folds her bony hands and waits until Molly has finished.

*

Molly feels the warmth of relaxation in her shoulders and neck. The tension is melting. She has neither won her bet nor lost.

She is relieved at what she sees. The woman opposite is both like and unlike the person she expected.

Yellow hair fading into white, dry with age like a pressed flower, curving around her head but short and crisp. It is as tidy and practical as anticipated. Sensible. Short enough to be manageable but still long enough to give a hairdresser something to work with.

Molly pictures her sitting in the salon beside Tesco Metro where the stylist flaunts fingernails with embedded diamonds, fanning a deck of cards. From beneath a towel, this woman explains to the stylist clearly what she wants.

'I want it to be sensible but wild too, because I have a wild side.'

Molly wants this to be true, even though she knows nothing about her.

'Bleached like Stella the slapper, madam?'

This woman would be far too polite to comment, but would say *'No'*, because she wasn't after attracting the boys, now was she?

Molly's eyes scan back and forth. They have had little nurture and are working overtime. They flit about this visitor's face like insects drawn to a lamp, hypnotised.

The woman's features are bony but not blunt. Skin more

white than pink, but not a shade so deathly that there's no life left in it. Active eyes behind plain red spectacles are neither busy nor at leisure, moving with smooth caution in their sockets without betraying surprise. They are not cunning like those of Stella, but generous, inclined to stretch with smiles, practised at signalling approval.

She is as lanky as Molly thought she would be, yet neither big nor broad. Cat-like, in a domesticated way. Her back would curve if you stroked her.

Her hands are the oldest part of her. Green veins and liver spots betray years that her face conceals. But there is grace about the way they glide, turning papers in a folder, placing themselves flat with confidence upon the table top.

She drinks a cup of tea. It is strange in an almost magical way. Where did she find the teabag? She speaks softly, and there is none of the noisiness or nastiness that Molly feared. Her honeyed voice comes down from the clouds. Inquisitive. Interested.

Her name is Eileen. Somehow, Molly knew that.

14

Eileen sits on her bed and looks out of the window across the land while there is still light. She chews slowly on bread.

This is her world. A life with little possibility spent in the shadow of a jaded husk shaped by blunt, pointless penitential routine. Churning of cream to make butter, picking stones from the hard soil, collecting eggs.

She appreciated sharing milk and ham with the neighbours and receiving them back in turn. She liked to house the turkey and geese at night away from the fox. She loved the haymaking on the farms in the summer, and bringing home the wheat and barley. But that was then. This is now. Long silences prevail in this lonely, haunted house.

She wants to excuse her mother. But she cannot.

What she never understood is why her father married this woman, although a farmer needs a wife. She is plain, her mother, weathered to a basalt stump. Her determined scowl stretches the leathery skin beside eyes like notches on a belt. It is the unmistakeable frown of a bad temperament.

Eileen's mother came from farming stock and knows no other way, but should have been a nun. So she has mortgaged the plot to God. It is a land lost to neighbours, a shrunken universe where there is little light from the sun. They have been left with a few potatoes, some hens, and a shortcut to a church in which to plead for mercy.

Eileen looks outside. The sky dozes beneath a grey blanket. Evening is approaching.

She lies back on the bed and pictures her father. She would never admit this to anyone, but he is becoming hard to remember. Eight years since. Sometimes she steals into the other room when her mother is at the priest's house. To ensure she does not forget. She wants to feel his arms pulling his special girl to his fathomless chest.

But it is Eileen who shall be the nun, a girl who gave up on God when he planted her father in clay. The Presentation Order does not perplex her. The Sisters were always kind at school. But her father hated the idea. She can hear his whispered brogue steaming in the dawn air, rising like mist from dewy grass.

'You'll not be joining the order, whatever she says. You'll stay on the farm with me.'

She smiles. His sparkling eyes glint with mischief.

Her mother did not defy him. The balance of forces was even. She cherished her church and controlled her kitchen with insane fervour. But it was a Murtagh farm.

And there was no mistaking his power. A human ox whose legs extended leagues. He was born of soil.

The means with which her father resisted her mother's insistent piety was his absence. He did not bridle at her haughty religiosity, he simply went out to tend the dog.

Eileen sees him now, as he watches her mother kneel to stare at Armageddon with stern prayer. He winks at his daughter as he is leaving. A silver apology to God.

*

She wakes at dusk, but dare not read a book under the light of a candle in case the light under the door alerts her mother.

I am meant to be asleep.

She lies silent as a corpse, looking through the window at stars whenever the clouds break apart enough to let through glimpses of space. She imagines her father up there, bronzed and healthy, a smile stretched across his manly face, tilling with a gleaming plough behind a godly horse. She hears him playing the side drum in the pipe band, and perhaps that lively sound invades her thoughts for a reason, reminding her that there is music in the world and not just the dour quietude of a bitter home.

There is a florin in the foundations, he once told Eileen. He knew so, because he put it there. He had helped to build the cottage as a boy, picking stones from the fields and lugging them back for the walls and hearth. Such physical toil fashioned the man he became, tall enough to reach the rafters, bulging with muscle. For his boyhood labours, he was given the honour of placing the coin in the damp earth. His own father looked on.

'It brought me good luck.'

He mused as he examined the sky himself, then tousled her straw-golden hair.

She feels his adoration like radiation. She was no strapping son to keep her father company and discuss the hurling, but he confided in her, the one he dared to love. That emotion was otherwise banished from their flat universe. A farmer needed a wife. That was that.

Eileen checks her wristwatch. It is inching towards nine and soon she will have to leave. She creeps towards the door and listens. The house is silent. She strains to hear the faintest sound of activity downstairs. All is quiet. But she knows her mother is still awake, poring over her *Lives of the Saints*.

The girl checks her purse in her pocket then rolls up her coat. She kneels on the bed and slips the latch from the window gently, then pushes the frame open as far as it will go. The bed creaks and she freezes, then relaxes. She throws her coat to the ground below and steps out of the window on to the slippery slate of the outhouse. She latches the window ajar so it does not flap and, with care, shuffles to the edge of the slate roof then slides down. She is thankful it is no longer raining. She gains a perch on the barrel to the side, and then she is on the ground and pulling on her coat.

She scrambles along the boreen dark with overhanging trees and through a hedge. A donkey snorts but she cannot see it. She rises and Aoife's house is in sight. The warm lights stand out in the wide sweep of blue-black sky spread over the hillock in between clouds to east and west.

Alone there in that landscape it seems as if this is the last family on Earth. Smoke idles from the chimney, picked out dirty white by a moonbeam. They are in the kitchen preparing. They are expecting her. She is breathless with excitement.

*

The cross-bar is a problem. The bicycle stretches the dress they had so carefully made across her calves. Fearing it will tear, she tugs it up her legs.

Careful what you show them, Eileen.

They cycle past the dairy then turn on to the good road leading to the parochial hall.

But those legs save the day. The Guards are checking that the girls have lights, and Eileen breaks their boredom. It is lucky, because the bicycle she had borrowed from Aoife's brother does not have a light. They let it pass with a whistle and a quip.

Don't be getting cold in your party dress, now.

It is not cold but heat she feels on her cheeks, yet in the moonlight no one sees her blush.

They walk up the hill then wheel down between the bog to the lingering scent of heather. In the distance the last light is exhaled in a disappearing silhouette of the mountains. But yellow floods from the door of the parish hall, a work in progress with a galvanised roof, yet electrified at last. The power is not sufficient for the band, and they have come equipped with car batteries for their amplifiers.

Rain has left a puddle on the floor, but missed the stage. The girls wheel their bicycles through the hall, trails of wet tyre tracks following them. They put their coats in the cloakroom, then check their faces. They smooth their dresses and join the others gathering on one side of the hall.

No one has heard of a glitter ball here, but Father Hanlon has dusted off Christmas decorations and strung glass baubles across the rafters. They sway in the rising heat of young bodies.

When he is satisfied that he has a full house, the priest takes to the stage with a self-aggrandising introduction, pointing to the leaking roof and talking of God's expectations and deep pockets. The band comes on, and there he is. Brendan. The girls scream and the unexpected sound takes everyone by surprise.

Father Hanlon calls for silence, insisting on a prayer, then positions himself beside the stage with his stopwatch. To avoid inflaming the passions, he will stop the music for two minutes after every three songs.

And with its holy guard on traffic duty, the band strikes up.

1

*B*leedin stench of tar.

Brandy heightened Stella's sense of smell and turned the tar into the wrong kind of passion. It invaded her hazy universe the size of a small caravan. Even if she had been able to think straight, she would not have been able to.

Stella sat at the table with a plastic cup and examined her bottle. She frowned. It was nearly empty.

She pulled her hair across her nose and took a deep breath, but there it was again. The smell of tar. That was his contribution to her life. Perfume of tar. He did not even say it right, if he spoke at all, because the word meant something else to him and she did not know what it was. She had no idea what went on inside that head of his, although like everyone else she suspected it was not much.

Mystery, she whispered, and pulled back the netting on the rounded window.

There was a form of beauty in the twisted mounds of rusting cars piled behind the galvanised railings of the breaker's yard. It was to do with the pattern of colours splashed in random between swirls of red oxide. To her, it spoke of freedom.

She watched the dog sniffing in the grass that had forced its way through the tarmac, shuffling from clump to clump. A mangy beast. An inhabitant of Sheerness. She felt a strong urge to kick the mongrel's rump, then Molly skipped across and crouched to hug the animal. Its tail wagged in simple joy, and Stella heard the child's muffled praise. The girl never talked like that to her mother.

Stella poured the last of the brandy into her beaker, suspending the empty bottle with too much effort to shake from it the last drop. There was nothing else to drink and she had no money. She decided to go back to bed and wait for a miracle.

She pushed herself up from the small table and stumbled

past the kitchen to the bedroom, her entire body weary from inactivity. She slumped face first on the flat mattress and felt the soft warmth of the eiderdown they had found rolled up in a cupboard. It stank of age and neglect, a musty murmur she barely noticed now. But it did not stink of tar, and for that she was grateful.

As she drifted back to sleep, indistinct sounds of Molly talking to the stray came through the wide window that spanned the rear of the caravan. The tone of a child frolicking, untouched by the passing of each day, took Stella back to a time that now existed only in her dreams.

She dreamt of Liam.

*

Stan stood there in a dream, as if suspended, watching an angry woman berate a man in a caravan beside a breaker's yard on the Isle of Sheppey. It was a scene he had observed many times from this vantage point, yet always when he did so it appeared to be the first time.

Cracked barks came from a snapping jaw. He could hear Stella, but was not listening.

... bleedin stench of tar again ...

Stan said nothing but his eyes said everything. They told her to leave him alone because he was tired and hungry and doing his best. Whatever it was that she could smell, he could not. The asphalt had done for his nostrils. Nor could he smell the alcohol on her breath and in her perspiration, although he could see the empty bottle. She needed a drink. This was nothing to do with the smell of tar.

He wanted to talk, to say something in between her complaints, but words failed him, as they always did. He had no money but the gaffer would pay him at the end of the week. As always.

Where are your bleedin balls? Ask him for cash up front.

This was confusing, The syntax tripped him up. What did

Stella mean? How would that work? It filled him with dread that he could not understand her.

Molly sat on the step and watched him struggling and could not understand why he could not understand. Stan knew she wanted chips because she had told him so. Stan knew Molly was angry, too, with hunger, because it was written across her childish face.

Stella watched, waiting for Stan to reply, a fuse burning. It was as if she had counted down from ten ... four, three, two, one, bang. She threw her empty bottle.

Like a bleedin kid!

He ducked in a reflex and glass exploded against the frame. Shards rained down on Molly and sliced her arm. The child screamed and danced and the dog took flight and Stella recited a verse of curses and Stan walked out.

He did not ask the gaffer for cash up front but took a job up north instead. For a month he grappled with the complex problem of how to understand Stella as he raked hot tar and breathed bitumen in Wolverhampton without noticing the smell. A strange image came to him one night of a woman like Stella from whose mouth poured hot tar at his feet. He was slowly sinking into it.

It was not what she said or whether it was true that mattered. It was how she said it. Stan simply did not understand.

2

*U*seless, *I am. Everyone says so. My mum says so.*

Molly stares at an empty cigarette packet on the kitchen floor, deep in thought. Eileen locates something imaginary on a piece of paper in front of her.

It doesn't say that here.

She turns the folder round for Molly to see, but the girl does not look, so Eileen turns it back patiently.

Don't go to school, do I?

Well, that's why they sent me.

It is overcast outside, drizzling, and the kitchen is darker now. Eileen stands to turn on the light, which does not work, then sits again. She sips her tea and looks at Molly above the rim of the cup. She does not stare, because she knows it will unnerve this creature whose appearance suggests neglect. She is all bones and Eileen wants to put some meat on her. She needs to find something to work with.

When you went to school, what was your favourite subject?

Molly does not want to think about Calton High. It is too painful. A prefabricated classroom bathed in harsh light populated by brutal children who feasted on pain.

She shrugs.

Couldn't do nothing, could I.

Eileen waits, the machinery of experience already diagnosing. She has seen very little, but she has seen plenty.

When I was your age, I wanted to be a teacher when I left school. What do you want to be?

Molly bridles, a faint tremor. The woman has taken her by surprise. The other schoolchildren talked endlessly about what they would do one day. Film stars, dancers, beauticians. They seemed to know what purpose meant. Molly has no idea where such thoughts came from. Outer space.

Me?

*

You can do anything. You can be an astronaut if you want.

Molly feels her face stretching, and it is unusual. It is a grin. That grin is hesitant, it flickers like a distant star. What Eileen has suggested is out of this world.

Don't be bleedin silly.

Molly smiles. Eileen smiles because the girl smiles, and this reaction is infectious.

Why not? Astronauts aren't just men, you know.

Molly swirls her finger on the table dreamily.

Anyway, I ain't American.

Eileen laughs, and her hearty bellow fills the room. It takes Molly by surprise.

You don't have to be a man and you don't have to be American. There's space enough for everyone. I could be an astronaut if I wanted.

Molly smiles again. Twice in one day. It must be a record.

Don't be silly.

Surely you're not saying I'm too old, now?

Molly blushes. It is precisely what she is saying.

Anyway, I didn't want to be an astronaut. I wanted to be a teacher. And so here I am.

Molly swirls her finger again. Eileen continues.

Do you know what I think?

Molly focuses on the cigarette packet, pretending to ignore her.

I think we should do some English.

But miss ...

It resonates, that word. It is the word children use for teachers. Molly realises what she has said and suddenly retreats to a whisper.

... can't do English ...

She notices that Eileen is fighting back more laughter.

... I'm useless.

And there's me thinking you wanted to be an astronaut?

Molly smiles again. A hat trick. Eileen weaves together her

fingers.

I have an idea. I want you to write down on that piece of paper there in front of you why you can't do English. Just one, short paragraph, easy. No one can see you. And while you're doing that, I'll make another cup of tea.

3

The gaffer at the depot knows Stan's a good worker. He turns up promptly, even when they start at five. He lugs his share without complaint. He does not mind the stink. He keeps to himself.

The gaffer also knows that Stan has a few slates missing, has to be paid in cash, and disappears for months on end before returning out of the blue.

The gaffer has only once turned him down. It was for his own good and it was because of Stella. She came out of the house in her nightdress and cursed the dumper truck as it passed through that forgotten corner of Roundwell. Those men are used to dirt, but not the filth that came out of that gob.

None of this was Stan's fault. She was three sheets to the wind and they knew it. The gaffer knew as well, but decided to create some space anyway. For the man's own good. Stan was expressionless when he told him, just gawping through those dead eyes that held so many secrets. The gaffer could not make him out.

'Sort your life out. There's a proper job here if you want it. But all this coming and going don't help.'

Stan disappeared again, that time to Folkestone. Did some driveways for Frankie. He set to thinking about what the gaffer meant.

'Sort your life out.'

Now he is in a caravan in Whitstable. He looks in the mirror at the cropped hair that he cuts himself and those piercing grey eyes that surprise him still. Why can't he sort his life out? He inspects his fading sweatshirt and checks the buckle of the belt that is always slipping down because there is no meat on the man either. He raises his hands and examines them, the scars and hard skin and ripped hairs and ridged fingernails. They are not weak. So what is wrong?

Stan suspects the problem lies in something his father once

said, one memory that he cannot forget that recurs to the noise of a fruit machine in the background. They were sitting in a pub that floated in a car park like a desert island in a puddle.

'You're no good, Stan. We've had enough.'

As he looks at himself in the mirror, Stan can still feel the roll of cash his father pushed into his hand before he turned and left.

4

*Y*ou'll butter it then put crumbs on. It's been de-boned *and filleted.*

You what?

De-boned. They've taken the bones out. Filleted, taken the insides out. So you don't do that. You do the spreading, buttering and breading.

What does that mean?

You flatten it, cover it with butter and crumbs, then stick it in a pack.

Don't sound like much.

You want a job, don't you?

Stella watches the greasy moustache jiggling as the parody of a man talks from behind a desk more battered than a slice of fish. His bloodshot and pitted nose remind her of someone who has stumbled and fallen on his face while trying to jump on a playground roundabout, careless, clumsy. She notices that his spectacles are held together with a sticking plaster.

She is on the street, and desperate. She has no money and every store for miles knows she is a shoplifter thanks to a chamber of commerce telephone tree. The warning about an itinerant thief has spread around the town faster than a virus: *'Some blonde bint in a pink tracksuit has been swiping chicken bakes, but we've got the measure of her.'*

She comes back to the man in the job centre, who has another question.

How's your back?

My back?

That's what I said.

S'all right. Why d'you want to know about my back? Want to see it? It'll cost ya.

He thought she was joking. She was not.

You can get a sore back doing this job if you're not careful. It's all about posture.

What?

Never mind.

He slaps the folder shut with self-importance, then clicks his pen and ticks a list on a clipboard he keeps in his in-tray.

Well, that's it. I'll let them know you're coming. Get there at eight tomorrow, sharp. Just wait at the front desk.

He reaches for the telephone then waits, his hand hovering. It is time for her to leave. It takes a moment for Stella to realise this and gather up her hoodie. She walks through the job centre as the other staff pull on their coats. She is the last punter of the day.

She does not need an alarm clock. The cold wakes her. The abandoned house is draughty and stinks. Drifters sleep there and it is littered with cardboard and soiled newspaper. It smells of sour urine. Swirls of graffiti adorn the walls. She found a discarded syringe. She wants a cigarette.

She pulls her tracksuit tight and waits for the light, then wanders through the waking streets to the seafront. It is raining. The wind combs her hair.

She stands outside the glass entrance to the fish factory hugging herself to keep warm until workers begin to drift in, then follows them and sits by the front desk, enjoying the heat. They shake rain from their umbrellas, and notice her as they file through to the factory floor. She hears machinery.

The receptionist offers her a cup of tea. It takes an hour for someone to come. A woman with a tight skirt and tighter face sits her at a desk and pushes a form forward, then lingers at the door.

I have to see the manager, just fill that in while you're waiting.

It is one form too far. It fills Stella with dread. She leaves. She never reaches the factory floor.

She sells something of herself for cash instead, ogled by drivers at a taxi rank who joke among themselves. She drinks brandy to kill the pain.

5

For the first time in her life, Eileen is asked to dance. She is spun off her feet. Pups yet to be creased from cutting turf on lashed bogs, saving hay and scything oats and barley cross the floor to put the question. There are even townies, visiting the hill folk.

A farmer's boy with two left feet stands on her toes, but he is pleasant and willing to chat. Another whose eyes roll with a life of their own is leery and asks her outside for air. She knows what this means, of course, necking in the dark along the hedgerow. She tells him she has plenty of air inside, and if it's kissing he's after then he'd better be proposing first.

Another buys her red lemonade, a Teddy Boy who has failed to smooth the curls in his mop. They stand beside the table with bread and cheese and ham fumbling for adult things to say.

The lads have been to Peadar's Bar to oil the pipes and hurried it down because there is no drinking in the parish hall.

When Deidre realises it is gone two o'clock she panics. They know their way in the dark to the road gate and the passage between the fields, but it is a hard slog against the sleet fired from the Atlantic sky. Aoife slips in cow dung, but the rain washes it away. They are drenched from head to toe by the time they reach the farmhouse.

Eileen hurries, nervous that her mother sometimes rises with the dawn from habit, and sure enough the sun is climbing in the east as she reaches the cottage.

She clambers back up on to the half-house and slips through the window. She listens carefully in the darkness of her room for sounds of life, her only concern to hide her wet clothes.

It is too late.

*

First comes the slap, a stinging rebuke that vibrates with an aftershock. Then comes the exorcism, a litany of reproofs plucked from the Bible. Then comes the clanking of the key in the lock. Finally comes the silence.

There is no food for Eileen that Saturday, and only a bowl of porridge on Sunday so she will not faint in Mass. She must stand at the back of St Bridget's.

'So that everyone can see what you are.'

Her mother announces at the kitchen table that enough is enough.

You will be joining the Sisters. You will sit down now and write a letter.

When she has finished writing, Eileen does not expect her mother to swipe the paper from her hands, fold it into an envelope, and march to the village to post it.

A threshold has been reached. Eileen senses that everything is about to change. Fear and excitement mingle in equal measure as she watches her mother cross the yard. Most of all, she is shocked at the confirmation that the woman, her own flesh and blood, cannot get her daughter out of her life fast enough.

6

I can't move. My hand is frozen. My fingers are clasped so tight they're bloodless white like greasy chicken. I can't feel the pen.

I stare at the blank sheet and it blinds me. The emptiness screams out what I already know, that I have nothing to say.

How do you write about nothing, an empty space, a story without a plot? It's like trying to see air, or describe white, or imagine what's inside a hole. There's nothing there.

My mind does not work. A bare cupboard. Nothing comes no matter how hard I force myself to think. I'm stupid, I'm certain of it. Stella says so. All the time. I can hear her now.

'Bleedin useless ...'

I know this to be true. She's asleep upstairs and although Eileen can't hear her snoring, the walls shake with her snorts. Her moody presence rattles me.

Eileen means well, but knows nothing. I can't just do what I want. I'm not like the others. I can't just pick up a pen and switch on my thoughts like a television that isn't broken. Didn't she notice? The lights don't work in this house.

I often wonder about this emptiness, as I lie in bed trying and failing to paint pictures in my head, lost and parched in the desert that is my mind. It's not that I don't notice things, it's that they don't stay noticed. I can't hold on to them long enough for them to mean anything.

I don't know why I can't do English. Mr Butler said I'm lazy. But I'm stuck, bogged down, trapped in tar. I'm so heavy I can't pull myself forward. It's a bad dream. I want to run away, but can't budge.

Yet this woman has come for me. For me. I must try, for her. It will be a mess, but I've left my bedroom and can't go back. I'll write the title. It's a plan at least.

Something snaps. My hand moves. I write some more. I

surprise myself.

I hold back my head to look at what I've done. My handwriting is rubbish. Ape writing by a monkey with a unibrow. Nonetheless, it's the first thing I've written for months. I have not let her down.

I've finished.

7

*O*nly came to get some stuff, then I'll get out your hair.
Stella taunts with a provocative smile. She waits for Eileen to respond, but the sound of movement in the room directly above draws their attention to the ceiling. Feet are planting themselves heavily on floorboards.

He'll be down in a jiffy. He don't bite.

That cackle again, but Eileen notes a quiver of false pride. A morsel of desperation. Accruing boys as trophies is open to ridicule, but if Stella does not do so what would she be?

Eileen sits down with her cup.

The sound of feet stomping down the stairs comes to the rescue. The face of a youth with acne appears around the door, his neck tattooed. Spiky brown hair refuses to behave. He appears to be shirtless.

When he sees Eileen, he is surprised. He gives the customary, silent greeting of the local tribe, flicking his head upwards in a kind of reverse nod, a gesture so subtle it forms an argot of motion that only the initiated understand. Eileen does not attempt to reciprocate.

You ready, Stell?

His voice is unexpectedly high. It ruins the effect. He is eighteen, but yet to be a man. Stella does not move. She does not turn to look at him. She is watching Eileen.

Just finishing my ciggie. Put something on.

She catches Eileen's eye and raises her own theatrically, exasperated, then turns to Rob and pinches her cigarette between two fingers, the nails glossed with garish peach varnish.

He turns abruptly and leaves. Eileen feels footsteps ascending the stairs, crossing the landing, then descending again. The front door opens and a rush of cold air sweeps into the kitchen. It is an entire language of movement. Stella chuckles. She thumbs after him.

That's Rob.

She leans back as if trying to turn her head through the kitchen door and shouts to an empty hall.

Close the bleedin door.

*

Eileen reasons with the pendulous weight of experience that in order to induce words not smeared with excreted antagonism she will have to tempt Stella to talk about herself.

So Eileen offers Stella a cup of tea, in her own kitchen. She risks a conversation. She needs to know why this bothered woman blows so hard on the embers of burning rubbish that is her life. If Eileen is Molly's ticket to the future, Stella is the bus station she is yet to leave.

Stella says yes. This takes Eileen by surprise. She had expected a jab from one of those toxic thorns that grow from the woman's mouth.

So Eileen pushes away the dirty plates in the sink to fill the kettle as Stella watches carefully, monitoring for signs of judgment. She places two cups on the table. Stella feels the urge to explain.

We're just passing through. This ain't our real home.

Eileen does not fully understand, but does not ask. She takes two teabags from her satchel and the carton of milk that she is now in the habit of bringing with her.

So why ain't you at school with the rest of them teachers? What you doing with a useless kid like Molly?

We aim to get them back into the classroom.

Stella rasps and lights up, crowding her hands around the end of her cigarette as if she has grown used to doing this in a blizzard. She mumbles with it pressed between her lips.

Good luck with that.

They sit there in silence, neither volunteering information. Eileen studies Stella's hands. They are trembling. She assumes this woman needs a drink, but the cigarette will do for now.

Are you from round here, Stella?

Stella laughs, but she is cautious.

Not likely.

She bites this answer off with her teeth, so that is the end of it. Stella will drink her tea and leave. She will give no more information. But then she does.

Been around, you know.

Eileen nods, almost with relief, grateful for that titbit. Stella pulls on her cigarette.

Mostly Kent ... Ramsgate, you know ...

Stella's eyes glaze and wander. She stares at the smeared wall behind the bin. It could have been a map.

... moved a lot ...

Her pupils flicker as they take in country roads and coastal caravan parks. There are motorway service stations and breakers' yards and council depots and the rutted back lanes of farms and fallowed fields. There are abandoned cars rusting in the sun, and driveways in need of asphalt, but also horses and dogs and sounds of children gambolling in the tall grass. And there is an abandoned quarry.

Eileen is no longer there but only the open sky and distance and the tinsel of light shimmering on the surface of the water.

... never had much time for school.

8

Molly did not name the dog. Stella called her a mutt. She was a bitch.

The bitch had a tan coat, lightly spotted on her hind legs, which were sturdy even though she was emaciated. She was hungry, but did not need much, and still had the energy to scavenge. Her elongated snout was sleek and she pinned back her ears with expectations that were never fulfilled. Her sweet glossy eyes were innocent of harm and as fragile as a doll. She lapped Molly's hand like an ice cream and span in circles. It was love at first sight. She appeared young but was world wise and knew the score. She had learned to navigate the good and bad people who washed up on that shabby coast.

They were on the Isle of Sheppey because there was a paving job and Stan knew where there was an empty caravan. Molly decided it was a holiday.

He spent the week raking asphalt, bringing home every day his exhaustion and the stench of tar that filled the volume of that small space and suffused their clothes and hair. Molly wanted chips but he was waiting to be paid so she sat on the doorstep and fed the mongrel scraps of bread. She laughed as the creature yapped for more and wagged her tail.

The animal slept with her on a mattress and brought in fleas so Stella kicked her and she yelped and cowered. She followed Molly to the field but was hopelessly lost in that open space and refused to fetch a stick. She looked at Stella on the couch, raised her snout above her head to smell the brandy, sweet on the skin, then looked at Molly and pushed into her with something like sympathy. Her ears riffled nervously at Stella's slurred recitation.

Then she was gone. Stella taunted Stan about the smell of tar and being broke and he did not understand so she threw a bottle. The mutt escaped at the speed of light. She had known Stellas before.

Stan disappeared so they left as they had come, suddenly, without a bag. Stella picked up her coat and told Molly to follow. The door was left hanging open. They had never set foot on the beach.

Molly wanted that stray. She needed to take her back to Roundwell more than anything she had ever needed. She had forgotten to name her.

But the mongrel was left foraging by the breaker's, her bed a culvert.

9

'*C*an't do English because I can't do nothing. Ask my mum. At school they took the piss. Don't see the point of English or nothing.'

Eileen takes another sip of wine and reads it again. The handwriting is surprisingly neat, nothing is crossed out, there are no smudges.

She pushes back in her reclining armchair, and uses the remote control to lower the soothing music from her sound system. Her attention is drawn to a shadow in her small garden, a branch nudged by a breeze as the light fades.

She hears her mother's voice, and is taken by surprise.

'You'll write it now, in your own hand, so they know you will be coming of your own free will.'

Her mother stands over her at the table, a small woman who rises in stature if her daughter dares to look her in the eye with anything other than obedience. Eileen wants to write that she will not be coming of her own free will. But she does not. She picks up the pen placed beside the paper. Her mother unfolds her arms and dictates.

'Dear Sister Agnes, it is with my firm desire to gain God's blessing that I write to request that you accept me as a novitiate ...'

Eileen fights back tears as she copies down the words. Her mother recites. She has been compiling this letter for years.

'... You will be familiar with my mother, Niamh Murtagh, of Duagh in County Kerry. I am ready to present myself at your earliest disposition and, with the grace of our saviour, work diligently to fulfil my vows ... yours in Christ ... sign it with your own name, girl.'

Eileen signs the letter and places the pen beside it. She sits, rigid, drained of any spirit let alone the holy version. Her mother snatches the note and folds it, then slides it into an envelope she has ready.

'Make sure you feed the chickens.'

A refrain in the music brings Eileen back. It is a relief. She sips her wine and runs through her plans once more. She has the money to retire. She will sell up and join Aoife. It should be simple. But a ghost haunts her as she imagines the silent fields of Kerry, the gentle lanes that meander between them. It is a phantom standing in a kitchen with its hands on its hips and staring at a crucifix.

Eileen knows she will have to confront this demon. A lot was left unsaid.

She becomes aware again of the paper between her fingers, and looks at Molly's paragraph. It is an unexpected source of comfort.

10

Butler's *Lives of the Saints*, Volume IV, October, November, December, *The Handy Reference Atlas*, which still has Ireland as a pink possession, *Ben-Hur: A Tale of the Christ*, Scott's *The Talisman*, *The Cruise of the Dazzler* by Jack London.

Eileen remembers the five books on the shelf of the other room. It is a crooked memory, like the board of the shelf itself, but a happy one. There are no ornaments above the fire.

She went in there, of course, when her father was alive, and sat on the floor by the fender beside the fire irons reading as he looked down from the battered armchair where he digested the newspaper under an oil lamp.

The smell of his clothes lingers, mildewed, dried earth in the fabric. The stained antimacassar, unwashed since antiquity. The light of the lamp swinging from a nail flickers on the uneven whitewashed wall discoloured with soot and mould. The eaves let in water beneath the thatch.

She hears the sudden snap of damp wood drying on the grate, and smells the steamy smoke rising from the turf. She pictures the holes in her father's socks, his long legs stretched as he warms his toes with a simple pleasure that speaks of honesty.

She sees his giant hands crossed upon his waistcoat as he drifts off, his eyelids heavy from work, his hacking chest slowly draining away the life. She hears the heavy breathing and the rush of air in his windpipe as he struggles to pump ripped lungs, bellows with holes.

These are the smells and sounds that have stayed with her. She watches her father drifting away, but smiling as he says goodbye.

He was old when he married her mother, but in the fields seemed ageless, a titanic force that trod the land with huge strides, able to sweep her up with palms the width of Ireland

and peg the giggling child to the clouds by her collar.

To her mind, he ploughed without a horse using just his legs, planted like trees. He worked forever without breaking a sweat, sweeping away all before him like nature itself. The truth, however, was that his frame was yielding. There was little love for all the toil, and even less reward.

Beside the armchair, an upturned wooden milk crate is his table. A fading picture of a happy cow smiles from its crooked slats. In that damp room its metal bands are rusting. Eileen imagined as a child that this was happening to him.

'Are you rusty, da?'

He smiles,

'I am, girl.'

She cannot forget the wheezing that he tries to hide as he reads to her from *The Talisman*. The depth of his voice, fissuring, conjures up the camp of the Crusaders in the Holy Land. He jokes,

'I am not Finbar Murtagh. I am Richard Coeur de Lion. And I have succumbed to an attack of fever.'

*

The dog ambles from the shed and Finbar scratches his friend's head with one finger. He clucks at the animal with kindness, for he loves his loyalty. Major is old now, and Finbar hopes he will make it through the winter.

The farmer observes the sky. There was mist earlier and although it has cleared the air tells him that it will rain. He is grateful it is cool, and still feels the night sweat that kept him awake sticking to his shirt. The silence is intact.

He crosses the yard and notes the chopped kindling in the outhouse. Behind its crumbling walls is the run and he knows that once she is up Eileen will feed the hens and collect the eggs, because she is a grand girl.

He has with him a sledgehammer and an iron claw because he intends to mend a broken fence that lets in the neighbour's bullocks. He starts for the field in brown overalls, tight at his shoulders, his former power implicit in his bulk, a button missing, wellington boots in need of replacing. He leans on the iron gate to survey the empty country, then takes the track beside the hill pasture as it rises into the gloom and emerges at a low plateau, a coppice either side where there is a stillness undisturbed by animals.

From here he sees the river winding between rocky fields dotted with clumps of gorse, sturdy cocks of hay still standing. If he were to wait long enough, a lark would fly out of the heather, or a snipe.

Behind him is the lane where little goes by except the occasional tractor. He sees the cottage, remote and alone. For a moment, he imagines that he can spy Eileen, and wishes she was with him for the company. He worries that she is lonely. He wishes he had a son, but only to keep her company. When he is gone.

He frets about her mother. A difficult woman. Time has not eased her discontent. They neither love nor hate, but exist in numb equilibrium. He pictures her in St Bridget's busy at prayer, the stale repetition bleeding it of divine purpose. Her cold hands are clasped, and he cannot imagine the touch of those fingers on his arms. Like expired fish.

The sky is wide and vast. A hawk circles sleepily, and he wonders whether God is watching at that instant and sees the space unfilled in the lonely heart of Finbar Murtagh. He asks why the woman does not see the church around her in these fields, the daily miracle.

The track slopes down towards the river field and on one side is ringed with a stone wall which he follows, and then he is at a wicket gate with its mat of scrappy clover and tangled sideburns of nettles.

He crosses the long grass and a rabbit darts into the bracken. He halts, and doing so makes him cough, and his throat fills with phlegm. He tries to correct his posture to make it stop, the iron taste of blood on his tongue, but the field is filled with the monotonous rasp of his hawking. He fears scaring the birds more than dying there.

It is a small field and the growth to one side is withering, exhausted bracken slumped between somnolent foxgloves. There is a badger sett somewhere.

To one side where the fence sags the land is sodden. The wire is slack, the lolling posts rot in the ground. He stops coughing. His chest warms as the scraping pain eases.

Clumps of rush have grown where the ground is waterlogged. Alders rise crooked by the riverbank. He takes a moment to skim a pebble and observe the tightly grassed banks on the other side. The birch have soared. There are blackberries with juice like the blood of Christ.

11

Eileen cannot bear it. She can no longer look at the pile of pans and plates partially obscuring the window to the small yard. She starts to busy herself with the dishes. Stella is not there.

She thinks better of it, and stops, looking for a drying cloth. She dries her hands on her sweater instead.

Well, now.

She pours hot water from the kettle into her cup, adds milk, puts the carton she has brought with her into the fridge, then sits opposite Molly at the table. She watches the girl eat cereal from a bowl.

That was a good start.

She threads her fingers together, waiting. She looks at Molly.

Would you read it to me?

The walls close in. It is a step too far. Eileen senses turmoil. The girl bridles. She grows white, colour draining from her cheeks.

Tell you what, we'll leave it for now. Instead, I'll read something to you.

Eileen reaches into her bag and pulls out a book. She fumbles for her glasses and places them carefully on her nose, then adjusts the distance of her head to bring the page into focus. She starts to read.

'Mr Utterson the lawyer was a man of a rugged countenance, that was never lighted by a smile; cold, scanty and embarrassed in discourse; backward in sentiment; lean, long, dusty, dreary and yet somehow lovable ...'

She reads for an entire five minutes without looking up. Then she closes the book and puts it down.

Molly pays attention, watching Eileen as she reads. The sheer novelty of having someone read to her has gripped her like a seizure. There is a long pause.

What did you think of that?

Molly says nothing, but nods instead. She looks at Eileen, but her eyes keep returning to the book on the table.

Did you listen carefully?

Molly nods.

Would you like to hear some more?

She nods.

"*But I have studied the place for myself,' continued Mr Enfield. 'It seems scarcely a house. There is no other door, and nobody goes in or out of that one but, once in a great while, the gentleman of my adventure ...*"

*

Eileen pushes the book across the table.

Molly freezes. It is not fear. It is an absence of belief.

Do I have to?

It's a good story.

Molly looks at the book.

What's the point?

Eileen remains silent. Her patience is a massif, an unmoveable weight.

Can't do nothing with English.

Eileen sips her tea. She puts down her cup.

There was a boy, at a dance, when I was your age. We had dances then, not like today, clubbing and all that. Anyway, this boy, he really fancied himself, and I knew he wanted to take me outside to, well, you know ...

Molly smiles.

What?

Eileen smiles.

You know ... kiss. Snog!

Molly takes a breath and giggles. Eileen makes a mental note. It is the first time she has heard this.

But I was having none of it. I wasn't going to be kissing that fellow for all the tea in China ... He had a face like a turnip. So

I had to get rid of him, hadn't I?

Intense anticipation.

So I said: 'I made a solemn holy oath to the priest there ...'

She points at the sink.

... because in those days the priest went to the dances checking up on everybody. And I pointed to him. And I said, 'I promised the good father that I would marry the first fellow at this dance to kiss me. So get on your knee now you big turnip and propose marriage like a real farmer in front of all these lads, because I'll not be going out there for a kiss, or anything else mind, until I've a polished ring on my finger.'

Molly gasps.

How old was you?

Sixteen. And do you know what he said?

Molly shakes her head.

Not a word. He ran like a scared cat. Because as you know there's not a young fella anywhere who wants to marry a woman who's the boss.

Now Molly laughs.

You see, you can be someone else when you want to. And you can use words to get what you want. That's what English is for.

Molly frowns with obvious concentration.

Eileen can as good as see the thoughts reeling in the furrows of her forehead.

12

The teacher says Stan is special, but they always knew that. Not like his brothers.

He has special ... needs.

His parents have maintained this silent secret from each other since the beginning of time, neither wishing to speculate whose blood is to blame. But they have their doubts, because his brothers are far from special. No one can control them.

He needs a bit of help ...

They listen to the teacher as she sits uncomfortably in the caravan, trying to appear relaxed, her longs leg pinned together awkwardly. It is never relaxing having to visit the scrappy end of Buckley Lane where there is no order and the children run wild and *dags* snarl at passers by with loyalty to this patch of dirt. But she is determined to do her job, to help a little boy more disadvantaged than the rest.

... with reading and the like.

She looks down at him sitting cross-legged on the floor and smiles, and he smiles back, because he likes this woman. He liked the way she sat with him alone at the school and read to him. He liked the pictures in the book. He liked the smell of soap.

You're special, aren't you Stanley?

He nods. He is special.

What she wants to say is that it will be difficult on the road to give the boy the help he needs. The school has the resources to do it, but it is a long-term proposition.

We have made progress. A teacher comes in from Grays. She's been doing it for years.

She turns back to his parents, and Stanley is disappointed. She explains that they can send him on a minibus with other children to the centre every day. They have a special programme to give the special children special help because they have special needs.

His mother looks at his father, her wan, leathery face with spider's web wrinkles less expectant than fearful at his response to whatever has warranted this intrusion. It will be taken out on the boy. And her. She feels her husband's rocky knuckles even now. She wants to love her boy, but he is such hard work, what with the other two, and that man, who has no patience for anything. She has no energy left.

His father stares out the window, blinded by the vacuum of whichever sky it happens to be, lost in wherever it is he will find the next roll of banknotes. The boys are old enough to help and that is the way of things. Stanley can use a shovel, can he not? He was helping his own father at that age, was he not? They cannot stay. They will go. They always do.

The teacher feels her resentment rising, as well as guilt for feeling it. They are unmovable, these people, with their ways, their bloody ways.

His father says nothing, and so neither does his mother, but she knits her fingers and the teacher notices, and knows he is saying no. There is a mother's anguish. She cares. They will pay her no heed.

The silence is as hard as her seat, and the teacher does not know what to do. She is used to being understood. She stares at little Stanley and hides behind her forced smile, waiting out the impasse. He picks his nose.

She knew all she needed to know when she saw the dirt under his fingernails, clinging there like matter from another planet no matter how often she sent him to the toilets. He left the tap on. The other children had an instinct. He was invisible, transient.

It took her days, and time she did not have, but she made him talk at last, his eyes glinting. He told her about the donkey.

'Gave him a turnip, so I did.'

*

Stan wants the donkey to come with them. He will feed it turnips.

'Where'll we put him, eejit?'

His older brothers mock him. He might as well be a donkey, he's that *tick*. They are growing up, and cruelty is expected. They flex muscles and whistle in that caravan now, eat the cupboards bare, disappear at night. Their mother can do nothing. The old fellow does not care, as long as they pay their way. He has his bottle.

But Stanley does not mind being called a donkey. He would like to live in a field.

He lies awake on the small sofa and tears stream down his face because he loves that donkey and does not want to leave. He pictures its long ears twitching to the hum of traffic, its lazy bray when he strokes its neck. Its eyes are kinder than any he has ever seen. Who will feed it turnips now?

It is not the donkey that carries Jesus in the book. It is grey, and the donkey in the book is brown. But Stanley knows it will go to heaven *annyway*. Because it is a donkey.

As they leave the site, he stares out the back window of the caravan until it finally disappears in the distance. His brothers are in the car with their da. He lets them drive. They go mad sometimes. They stole a car then burned it. They brought home cash. The old man bought a bottle.

Stanley wants to know why he is special. What it is like to go in a minibus.

He pictures the teacher driving. She smiles at him in the mirror. He tries to remember the stories she read him, but cannot. He recreates her voice. She uses funny words. They talk like that, those people.

Another teacher, a big man, told him to turn the tap off. He asked Stanley if he was born in a barn. Jesus was born in a barn. And later rode a donkey.

Stanley could tie the donkey to the caravan. It would run after them wherever they went. He would feed it turnips. Why don't they understand?

So he was sad when his father said he was going for petrol.

That was all he said, but Stanley knew they were leaving. A small voice inside him wanted to speak. He wanted to stay.

His father slapped his brother round the head before they left.

'Tievin's tick if yous get caught, so.'

Stanley likes the silence of the night. The traffic does not drone in the background like it does in the day. It is easier to think. He imagines the donkey there now, tied to the back of the caravan in the layby. It does not mind the traffic, because it grew up in a field by the motorway. It sleeps standing, and snorts in the morning when it wants its turnip. It tries to talk but cannot because it is a donkey.

It is in its field now, a long way away. But he knows that one day he will find it. Because he is special.

13

The slide, the slide, oh the slide.

I'm goin on the slide first.

Stella runs so fast she glides. Her feet do not touch the ground. She sees it passing beneath her and flaps her wings. Liam follows her, but slower still, because he is older and more wary. He looks around, through the windows of the empty school, across the deserted playground and through the railings to the houses across the street, to check for signs of life. Sunday torpor has suspended the village in a cocoon of sleepy calm. There is nothing but hush.

Long shadows stretch from the school building across the play patterns printed on the ground in pink and yellow, a green alphabet snake, a numbered trail. Heat from the sun is already rising from the surface and they will roll on that later, absorbing the energy, oblivious to the sound of their own laughter.

He catches her at the steps, and pushes his way in and up.

Me first, I found it.

She clucks, but does not care, and follows him up. He stops, breathless, at the top, which seems higher than were they to be climbing the big oak by the caravan in the field. He surveys this lost world that they have discovered.

Liam positions himself, straightens his legs, checks his destination, then pushes and slides, disappearing like light down the polished stainless steel. Stella screams with delight to see her brother's back vanish from sight, then scrambles up and into position to watch him rolling off at the bottom with a gargle of glee in a bundle of dirty knees and unrefined vigour.

She shouts,

Me now, coming do ... o ... o ... wn,

and as she travels she is lost for breath and the acceleration takes her into a moment of slow motion in which the entire wonder of the world in all its fuzzy confusion is revealed. There are no caravans or school buildings or playgrounds here, just movement purified, and the glorious interference it creates in the fabric of the universe.

Liam is gone, spinning a red roundabout at an accelerating pace until his hands can no longer catch the bars as they race past and he runs with it, dragged along until he hops on and she sees his face then back then face then back. The grin rushing past her is wider than the sky. She implores him to stop so she can climb on with him and he does, then she sits and he spins and they are off, together, in a vortex that gyrates their minds, a welcome dizziness.

Then they are off again to the climbing frame, and swings, and mounds and tunnels, a mountain wall. Liam favours the space frame, suspended upside down from the bars, enjoying the feel of blood rushing into his head. Stella pretends to be a queen, surveying her kingdom from the battlements of a mock castle. They run and roll and shout and laugh. They rest under a tree and sit on a bench at a table, hungry and thirsty now, but not enough to stop. She follows him like a pet, slowing down and speeding up in sibling concert, happy for the adventurous boy to take the initiative, copying when she can.

Liam boasts proudly about his discovery and how he watched the children playing, and they speculate wildly about what happens in schools and the food that is served in the canteen, chips and chops and puddings.

They play until the caretaker turns up, alerted by a neighbour, fulminating, his red face fit to burst before he has even descended from his battered Volvo, spoiling for a fight, outraged at the notion of children putting a playground to use on a lazy Sunday when there is no one there to care.

But by then it is too late. They have had their day. They screech at one look of the angry man and run and are gone across the field through the copse with memories still twitching in their tired muscles.

It is nearly sunset *annyway*.

*

I want to go, mammy. I want to go with Liam.

Stella stands outside the door clenching her little fists. She stomps in the mud in bare feet like a Shetland pony at the horse fair. A dirty blonde little flicker in the twilight dressed only in knickers but oblivious to the cold. There is a residue of sugar from sweets around her mouth to which has adhered soil from the field. Her eyes shine with liquid emotion, always on the verge of something.

Liam isn't goin you little gobshite, now get in here 'afore I belt your ear.

Her mother reaches for her but the tyke dodges and looks up at her brother watching from the window of the caravan with that grin sliced across his freckles, forever that grin.

He only said he's goin because he ain't goin.

I want to, I want to.

Her mother is exhausted. The woman's greasy black hair flops across her haggard face, weary from the bother of it all, and she is of half a mind to leave Stella there in a littered field in Lincolnshire. The brat can fend for herself and be devoured by the creatures of the night for all she cares. The woman looks up at Liam, the source of all the trouble, staring down at them like the little king that he is. She tosses at him the expression she has stocked to signal a threat of retribution, although he calculates that she will forget because she always does beneath the weight of her chores.

Tell her you lying smear or I'll ...

He slams the window shut and disappears inside. There are few places to hide in a caravan, but he knows she will run out of patience looking and he will escape her clutches. He is canny, that boy.

She has had enough. They will be the last to leave the field. The others are already up the lane and will be on the dual carriageway. They will lose them.

Give her what for ...

A growl slushes from the window of the Range Rover and spills across the stubble of cut wheat worn bare by coming and going.

... or I will.

Stella hesitates. She fears her father's threats, even though he is weak and put upon. Her hesitation is just enough for her mother to pace across with menacing purpose and grip her little arm in the vice of her bony hand. The woman yanks her back towards the caravan door. The girl screams loud enough to wake several generations of dead.

Darkness is descending like a fog, concealing mounds of rubbish that mark where they have existed these past months, but the chrome door of a washing machine glints in the last blink of light before a cloud shuts out the day.

No one here gives a toss what you want you little cow ...

She hauls the child by one arm through the door and throws her to the floor. Stella falls heavily with a thud and screams again.

... annyway, what use would their school be to you, it'd only make you better at the nottin' you're good at already. Now get to sleep. There's no food for the both of yous.

The engine of the car roars into life and the woman slams shut the caravan. Stella crawls along the clammy linoleum into the tiny bedroom. The door shuts with a click behind her. Liam hides under the cover. He has made himself as flat as he can, and she knows this trick well because he has used it so often. It is the last place his mother will look.

She wipes mud from the soles of her bare feet with her hands, snivels, then climbs in alongside him. He rolls over to face her in the dark.

I only said I wanted to go because they play footie, I saw them. Girls don't play footie. Annyway, Da said fock off. He said over his dead body. They hate us, he says. Annyway, Da says we have to do what Big Bob says and if not we're on our own.

Stella sniffs.

I want to go to school.

Da says we don't need school. Can't teach us nottin'.

They've got a slide.

Big Bob says we got to leave.

Stella begins to sob. She rubs her eyes with her dirty hands. Liam changes the subject.

Mammy's having a baby.

I know.

Comes out from between her legs.

Ugh.

Goin' to be a boy ...

What if it's a girl?

Don't want a girl.

Stella remains silent. She tries to look into Liam's eyes to know what he is thinking, but it is too dark. But then the room lights up as they turn with a jerk on to the dual carriageway. Headlights slide across his face, but miss his eyes.

Da says girls are trouble.

He prods her playfully.

Trouble.

Not.

Are.

She pokes him and he giggles, and they laugh until they sleep.

14

Rob is there again, shirtless and painted. He hovers by the kitchen door as Eileen enters. He is only half dressed, unless you count tattoos.

Eileen is embarrassed. She averts her eyes from his scrawny form, which rises like white bread out of his baggy jeans. His belly button is the knot in a party balloon that has been insufficiently inflated, and his ribcage the spindly fingers of two hands clasping him from behind. He is either underfed or too busy slithering up and down drainpipes to take in a meal or two. His head crouches between shoulders permanently hunched and dotted with spots. His back arches so much that any clothing on it is likely to slide off. This helps Eileen understand why this youth always appears to be shirtless. She wonders if this is how he wanders around the estate.

Either way, she is the opposite of impressed with his body, although Stella clearly is. A strange, smoky lust for this skinny boy shines in her otherwise dulled eyes.

Eileen smiles as she wipes her feet. He withdraws upstairs with a sleek, effortless choreography that suggests superior climbing skills. The saying *'He'd steal the shirt off your back'* was invented for the shirtless Rob.

In the kitchen Stella sits, immobile, smiling dreamily. The dishes are piled high.

Eileen has planned another conversation. She has attempted to map out all the possible directions in which this can go, but Stella is wholly random. Predictability contains too many syllables. Therefore, Eileen applies her instinct for psychology, learned at the foot of another unpredictable, difficult woman. She puts her satchel on the table.

How are you, Stella?

Could do with more cash.

Eileen fights back a smile.

15

I sit with the book on the sofa. I read under the poor light of the streetlamp. I'm alone but I can hear Eileen's voice reading to me.

There are so many lines in pencil on the page that it looks like a railway junction. Eileen told me to underline the words I don't understand.

'Just write down what you think is happening so far. Tell me what's going on.'

It's hard to know. But I'm ploughing on.

My eyes are unexpectedly tired. The book is called *The Strange Case of Dr Jekyll and Mr Hyde* and it's good. There's a creepy picture on the cover, but I ain't scared.

I read the first chapter, the one what Eileen read to me. It's called 'Story of the Door', and I think about it a lot. I look at the door of the front room. It's shut and I feel happier in this room than I've felt for weeks. I'm enclosed within a world that I'm creating. Pictures form and I don't have to force them.

I think about my bedroom door. I've decided to leave it open. Being at home is a drag. I'm bored stiff. I *want* to read the book that Eileen gave me.

I think about Stella upstairs moving to and from the bathroom, opening one door then another, never standing still, waiting for Rob to give her money, always waiting. It's quiet upstairs and I don't know if she's there. I haven't heard her door opening or closing for ages. Even when Stella is there, she's not.

I read about the door that My Hyde went through. I think about how bad he is. I wonder what has happened to make him like that.

I reflect upon my promise to Eileen. I promised to read the chapter. The words are hard but I've already finished it. I'm reading on.

I wonder what Stan is doing now. I wonder if he's ever read

a book. He doesn't seem the type. I don't think I'll ever know. I know that Stella hasn't.

I want to know why Eileen brought this book. There are lots of books to read and I'm curious why she chose it. I wonder whether it's her favourite. I make a note to ask her.

16

Eileen never found out what was her da's favourite book. She never asked him. Nor did she ask what was his favourite colour, animal, song, prayer.

But she knew his favourite person, because he told her constantly in the field and yard and when she was collecting eggs and when they were walking to Abbeyfeale on a silent morning before he had bought her a bicycle and before he retreated to the bedroom.

'Don't be silly, da. I have to be your favourite, because there's no one else.'

He roared with laughter when she rolled her eyes like that and looked quite the little woman even though she was only a sprite, but inside he knew he had let her down. She was alone. He was all she had. Apart from her mother of course, but the woman did not know how to love.

'What about Major? Maybe he's my favourite?'

Then he would bend down and pull the gleeful setter's muzzle into his knees and stroke him all the way down his back with such pressing attention that the dog would crumple into the man with ecstasy.

When Major died, it was as if a light went out. His shadow. A better friend than the woman he had married.

Of the five books on the shelf, Eileen later speculated on her way to school that her father's favourite was *The Cruise of the Dazzler*. This was not just because it was the most exciting adventure she had ever heard and the only book he had read to her from cover to cover, but because her da said he knew a man called Joe Bronson once and she imagined it must have been the very same fellow who had run away to sea because school was so dull.

She pictured Joe in his hobnail boots, still ill-fitting because he was still growing, lashing the boom of the mainsail on the sloop in a raging storm, his wet hair pasted across his face by the gale. She imagined herself beside him, almost hanging from a grommet as the wind tried to fling her on its shoulders effortlessly like her da.

When her father read to her in the poor light, he strained his eyes to focus on the tiny printed words and, although she did not know it, he missed many of them and so filled in the gaps with his own plucked freely from the vocabulary of the gates and markets. When the going got rough and his eyes were closing against his will, he simply made it up.

'He was a great big amadán, that fella, with dirty fingers the colour of drisheen.'

Eileen would not know the difference until years later when she read the book again, amazed to discover that Joe Bronson was from San Francisco, not Tralee.

17

M olly's face burns with the embarrassment to come. Apprehension surfaces like pollution. It sticks to her skin and she itches. It is how she felt when waiting for Mr Butler to hand back homework.

She tears the sheet of paper from the pad. She coughs as she hands it to Eileen.

Eileen senses the girl's discomfort and reaches over to touch her hand.

I can read it out here for the both of us, or at home later. What do you want me to do?

Molly does not object, but that is because of paralysis.

Eileen pushes her glasses up her nose and begins to read in a volume low enough to keep a secret.

'The Strange Case of Dr Jekyll and Mr Hyde ... There are lots of words in this book that I don't understand. That is because no one never taught me them words. For example, there is a word on the first line, it says countenance, and I don't know what that means. So that makes it hard to read this book. There was a bloke in my class at school who knew every word under the sun. I bet he knows what countenance means, cause he was really smart. He was one of them what never picked on me neither. Anyway. This book starts about a man called Mister Utterson. He drinks gin, as far as I can tell, because the way these words are written is very strange. I think it is very old fashioned. I don't mind that, in fact I like it to be honest because it sounds posh. My mum drinks gin and the rest so they got that in common, her and Mr Utterson, although she prefers brandy most of the time, and that's more pricey. Anyway. He is tall and seems nice, and is a lawyer and I know what that is because my mum had one when she was up for shoplifting. His name was Mister Edwards. He was nice. He told her to stop drinking.'

Eileen smiles broadly. Molly had read the first chapter. She had thought about what she had read. It warmed her.

This is great. Well done.

Molly's eyes widen in shock.

You really think so? Why's it great?

Eileen does not know where to start, so she starts where she always does.

It's great because you have put your feelings into it. You have described what you are thinking. For example, look at what you have written here ...

She takes a pencil and underlines a clause in Molly's work.

'I like it to be honest because it sounds posh.'

Eileen watches as Molly levitates. If she had been a balloon, she would be rising to the ceiling by now such was the value of this small jewel of praise.

You see, even though you found it hard to read, you stuck at it, didn't you?

The smile on Molly's face is so wide it could crack the walls. It is as wide as a bookshelf.

They discuss what she had written for the remainder of the class. Eileen tells her what countenance means and asks her what kind of person she thinks Mr Utterson was. They look at the description of him and agree that he was a serious man who liked helping other people. They did not discuss what he had in common with Molly's mother.

18

S tan knew what Stella was up to. He said it was not their way, although neither of them knew what their way was. It was what his father would have said.

At first they shared the caravan and he had work spreading tarmac. They bought food. But Stella did not stop, especially when he disappeared for a week to the Midlands. To pass the time, she drank.

He put up with it because he did not see it. Nor did he understand what was really happening. Then Molly came along and there was work emptying the bins in Roundwell which meant he came home at night. He gave Stella money again. She spent it on booze again.

It lasted ages, that bin job, and the gaffer had a soft spot for him and helped him get on the housing. They had never lived in a house and they did not know what it was for and how it worked. Stan did not know where sofas came from, but found one on a skip. He sat there in the empty front room imagining this is how the settled people lived. But even his dreams were in motion, and when he sat there he never sat still.

It was why one day he dropped the bins and took a paving job in Swindon and disappeared again. Stella was left to deal with the social worker. Molly must go to school. Stella told her where to go. Molly went by herself.

The police brought the child home at midnight. She was walking around the shopping centre and did not know where she lived.

'I live in a house.'

The social services said they would take her, but did not account for Stella. Molly watched from the upstairs window. Two policemen and two social workers formed a huddle on the pavement, where Mrs Nally came out with her lumps every day, and decided that arresting this woman was more trouble than it was worth.

When Stan eventually returned, he was locked in silence. He buried his frustration because of Stella's tongue. It was sharper than a shovel. His escape was his labour, asphalt and fetid bins that he could not smell. These things gave him motion.

But he watched Stella fester.

And when she started to bring home other men again, the rage became unbearable.

19

A   funny little mouse was chased by an angry cat who ran into the television and made a hole in it. The mouse was brown and the cat was black.

I remember it clearly. It was the last thing I watched on the screen in our front room. When I came down in the morning, there was hole in it.

It comes to mind because I have asked Eileen what she read when she was young.

Everything I could get my hands on. We didn't have a television.

We don't have a television neither. Stan made sure of that. Or rather Stella. I haven't the foggiest idea what happened, but I'm certain it went something like this: she's drunk, he's tired, she's tongue-lashing him, he's tired, she's cruel, he's tired, she goes too far, he kicks the telly, she barks, he leaves.

 Eileen is surprised when I tell her.

It worked once, don't get me wrong, but it got kicked in.

I put down the book that we have been discussing. Eileen folds her fingers the way Mrs Nally might if a child suddenly burst through the bedroom wall and she was sitting in her curlers.

I was the only kid at school without a telly. So you wasn't the only one Eileen.

You're not missing much, trust me.

I do not hear her, because I drift. I hear the others at school, mocking me, pulling grotesque faces to evoke a grimy pauper, sticking their tongues beneath their lower lips, shaking their heads, laughing hysterically. I return.

Stella watches it anyway, even though it's broke.

It is a strange observation, and I can see Eileen picturing my mother sitting brain dead in front of a smashed television, the only thing on the screen her reflection. It makes sense.

How did it get broken?

Dunno. Some fight, 'spose.

Eileen does not press. She waits.

Stan got angry with Stella. They was always fighting. She's a bit like Mr Hyde, 'spose.

I pin my eyes on the distance and try to imagine Stan's foot going through the screen. And then something within me volunteers more. I need to tell Eileen about my father.

He ain't bad, Stan. Speaks funny, like you. But he was never here.

Eileen offers a sympathetic smile.

So where's Stan now?

20

It fills the emptiness, the church of St. Bridget.

If Niamh Murtagh keeps herself busy in it, then everything is automatic and her body and mind are not her own. She does not have to think. A vessel tossed in a sea with no land in sight.

There is plenty to do, no task too menial for the faithful.

Polishing the brass, and God only knows there's enough of it, watering the flowers on the altar, and God only knows where the florist in Listowel comes by so many of them in winter, chipping away the candle grease, and God only knows why there's more of it than there ever was in the candles, scrubbing the chancel tiles, and God only knows where the mud comes from when only Father Hanlon comes and goes and his shoes are never dirty so saintly is the man.

Then there are the missionary leaflets to replace and the stitching of the cassocks and all this before she even starts on the presbytery and the good father himself always answers the doorbell for the Lord has denied the suffering man a proper housekeeper and so she does everything she can to ease his burden. It is her penance and will be her redemption. God will see her proximity to a man cut for this cloth, who condemns with ardour the threats of a leisurely life to his orderly church. A man of the parish who caters for only the faithful, ingests their sins, delivers absolution, generously shares the Host.

The good father knows that. She can tell from his tone at confession. She thinks about that as she waits. Then, when he taps the grille and tells her by her name to speak up she knows he is talking to Niamh Murtagh herself. The very same girl who learned all her lessons from the Sisters. Never to talk to the postman or dance in the hall or whisper songs about kissing.

Her knees ache. She has finished her churchly labours but wants to stay there alone and pray some more. The silence is soothing. Her chants fill the void that stretches from the back pasture to the cottage.

She knows, then, that it is divine this pain she suffers. It is not the infinite desolation of a farmer's wife who should have been a nun but missed her vocation. If she concentrates on the words, they take on meaning, and this gives her purpose. She may be a farmer's wife, but she is a Nazarene treading on palms beneath the burning sun of the Holy Land, her eyes open to the heavenly light.

She looks at the dolorous face of Mary, and in between thinking she would dust it tomorrow but what it could really do with is a lick of whitewash, she tries to imagine from the serene alabaster what God's mother was thinking. What was it like to have been part of a story? To have kissed the cheek of Jesus? To have ascended?

Exalted, she feels her arms spreading as she is lifted. Her legs are weightless. She hovers, in the rafters, looking down, and knows her work here is not in vain. A dwindling farm in bleak Duagh. There is a reason.

She is back in her body. The pain in her knees has gone. She studies the crucifix, thankful for St Bridget's with its brass, flowers, tiles and candles. The generous smile of sweet Jesus, his face so understanding she wants to kiss him.

The church itself is heaven in a way.

*

She scrapes Finbar's chair away from the oak table to sweep the uneven floor, then pushes it back when she is done, and does the same with the others.

She kneels on the cold stone and prods the broom as far as it will go beneath the white dresser, which dominates the kitchen. There is little dirt to pull into the dustpan because she does this every day and there is no time for it to gather, but the routine is a rite and must not be missed.

The dull bump of wood against the pale green skirting board is the only sound in the kitchen. She has not yet tipped anthracite into the stove and pulled out the damper, and there is no cracking of flames.

Niamh hears the faint rattle of cutlery in the drawer as she moves the brush beneath the dresser. *Old Moore's Almanac* wobbles ritually on its shelf. She stands and straightens her stiff back to lay the book flat so that it does not topple, then pulls the brush free.

There is almost nothing in the dustpan, but she empties it on the coals anyway.

Then she closes and latches the window she had opened to let in the cold air, and puts the broom and dustpan in the scullery. The floor shines with red Cardinal polish. She stands at the threshold and examines the whitewashed walls and the ceiling crossed by dark beams. It will soon need painting, but he will not be able to do it. Eileen will have to help, and she will not tolerate her complaints.

She half expects to hear the latch rising and to watch him taking off his boots, but remembers that he will not.

She checks the coal in the fire pit and blows it into life, then scoops more on top. She adjusts the damper and soon the heat is rising, and she pulls down the falling crow and places the kettle on top. She will take him a cup of tea and a soda bun. He has lost his appetite.

She tests the hob and feels it warming, then opens the wrapped beef and teases out the fat with her fingers. She slices across the meat and then dusts it with flour, scrapes potatoes, cuts a cabbage. She is not inclined to make dumplings for it will only be the two of them eating and Eileen nibbles like a bird. She cuts dripping from a bowl in the scullery and dabs it into a saucepan on the hob, now hot enough to brown the beef, then places them in the casserole.

The kettle boils and she pours water into the teapot, then puts it on a tray with a bun on a single plate. She carries it up the stairs and hovers outside the bedroom door until she hears wheezing.

21

The foyer of Roundwell leisure centre is empty except for a bleak reception desk that looks as if it may have been taken from a ship. I have the feeling of too much space expanding around me as I walk across and take in the high ceiling with its bolted metal joists. Large glass panels separate the outside from the inside. They look in on nothing. There is no sense that this is a space waiting to be filled.

There is an abstract artwork on the wall behind the reception desk that in all the time I have been bringing pupils here I have never grown to like. I think it is made out of recycled trash, which has been painted different colours to conceal the reality. In a brief tic of thought, I hope that it is sanitary. The receptionist seems bored, she stares out across Roundwell waiting for nothing. She sees movement, and it is me, and she pulls out a smile she has in stock. She knows me.

I peer through the double doors into the library. It is silent, even though it is at the heart of the estate. This is a sports centre with a small library appended to it. It is not a library with a sports centre appended to it. The library could be empty, although when I squint I see people in there. I strain to focus. I see an old man sitting at a table reading a newspaper. He has his back to me. He is not Molly.

I look at my watch, then reflect on why. Force of habit. I have put no time constraints on Molly Path and nor do I want to. There will be only one time that matters in our relationship, and that will be the exam that concludes it. I like that sense of timelessness surrounding her. It frees her in a way.

I glance across the car park through the large glass plates of the centre and see her. She holds her head down as she shuffles forward, as if hiding, her head bent to conceal her face. She pulls open the door and comes to me, clutching the book I gave her. She takes in the place, interested in her surroundings, but surreptitiously through stolen glimpses that give nothing away.

Have you been here before?

Molly shakes her head without a hint of embarrassment. She has lived on the estate for years, but she has never been here.

I wanted to come. To get out.

I smile to thank her for that unexpected crumb of support, and open the door of the library. Inside, I now see a few young mothers sitting with toddlers reading playbooks in the children's section. There is also the old man reading the newspaper.

The librarian looks up from the desk as we enter and also smiles with recognition. I am something of a regular. The Mudlark has an arrangement to use the building for individual tutoring, and I have been there many times. Part of the furniture, almost.

I lead Molly to a table that I always use between rows of books towards the back, away from the sight of others. Now she is looking around carefully, interested in her surroundings. She detects the calm, it envelops her. She does not feel exposed.

Better than school.

I am pleasantly surprised again. Molly wants to be here. It is a relief, because this is the first time she has ventured out, and she has done so alone. I hope that this class goes well. I take my papers from my satchel. Molly puts down her book and sits.

I find it is a good place to work, Molly. A good atmosphere.

She nods, although there is a hint of anxiety in her smile. I read her face and I know there is a struggle going on. In truth, I had expected her not to come, or perhaps to set out but never arrive. I had prepared myself for another wasted day, and for trudging back across the estate to the house to start again.

But now I am reassured. Molly did not run away. She is coming back, and I realise that this is brave. Was I as brave?

I am aware that this is a watershed.

22

It says clearly: '*Danger. No Swimming*'. The children ignore it.

It even has a picture of a stick person swimming in wavy lines of water with a red line across it, but Liam drapes his clothes on that.

He is determined to dive in from the only outcrop that remains in the otherwise sheer walls of the quarry, scarred from years of mining. Tufts of buddleia cling to the rock.

He has mapped it out in his mind. He will swim to the centre and then back and there are enough dispersed rocks at the foot of the outcrop to slide along before climbing up.

The thought of a twenty foot dive that has him slicing into the water sharp as a knife fills him with unbearable excitement. It is the thrill of fulfilling something he has set his mind on since they pitched their caravans beside the derelict depot of an abandoned stone works. He is driven by a need more powerful than all the caution that could possibly be had were his jumpy mind one day to stop, step back, and think, for goodness sake.

He does not stay still and must be in motion. His mother does not understand where he gets his energy from, because she lost hers years ago. He has no one to play footie with, because Stella does not want to and, *annyway*, girls don't play footie. He will burn it off swimming, so he will.

Come on, chicken.

He clucks like a bird at her and flaps his elbows against his ribs. She shakes her head as she watches him strip down to his underwear and shiver. The afternoon sun has lowered and a rod of cold is swiping at the air. It wraps itself around his skinny white belly but he does not care. It is an adventure.

Wait till I tell da. Champion diver.

Liam edges to the tip of the outcrop and examines his toes curled at the rough edge. Stella stays back, away from the drop, fearful. She does not like the water. She wants to go back to their caravan. She follows him everywhere. But today she will not.

C'mon Liam, let's go. You are'dnt going to, you are'dnt.
Am so.

23

A cog turned and I felt it moving. It was not like school. It was better.

Eileen asks me to write down my ideas about the place the author was describing with as much feeling as I can.

Try and give it some atmosphere. Try to take me there by painting a picture.

As she reads the newspaper, I notice her looking at me from the corner of her eye, listening to the scratching of my pen.

I'm being watched, I know that. It's something I'm used to. There's no escape in this life. At school, the others watched me all the time. That's what I think of. Eyes. Millions of eyes, finding fault, looking for an excuse, judging me, sniffing at the weakness.

When I entered the class, they knew I'd entered the class. When I'd not done my homework, they knew I'd not done my homework. When I went to the toilet, they knew I'd been to the toilet. When I skipped lunch because I had no dinner money, they knew I'd skipped lunch because I had no dinner money.

But I welcome Eileen watching me, even if she is trying not to. In fact, I want her to watch me, to notice what I do, to think about this. It is as if she is thinking about who I am, and I ask myself, *'Who am I?'* and apart from my name and my disgusting face and the sore on my heel I realise that I do not know who I am. I am not the sum of all my parts, but the subtraction of all my parts. There is even less there than it seems. I'm the girl with the smile in reverse. Perhaps Eileen knows something that I do not. Perhaps she knows who I am.

These thoughts distract me. My pen is motionless and I will my hand to move but it does not and I realise that it is frozen, so I reach across with my other hand and grab my wrist and force it to move. This is a strange thing to be doing. It would seem that Molly Path cannot control her own hand. I ask myself if this happens to other people. It cannot just be me. I wonder whether it has ever happened to Eileen. I find myself writing again.

It turns out that Mr Utterson already knew someone else who lived in the house that he had seen Mr Hyde enter. At least, I think he did. I'm not certain, because the language confuses me. I ask Eileen, and point to the sentence that I think is important. She nods. I'm correct, and elated.

Don't know why we never done this book in class.

You would have if you'd stayed. The rest of your class will be doing it now. It's in the GCSE.

Eileen puts her hand on her heart.

So the question is ... shall we keep going?

A door has opened.

*

I stand in a foggy London street. It is the olden days. The buildings crumble and are dirty. Tramps slumber like discarded litter in the shadows. They strike matches on the wall. There is a dark door with no bell.

I picture that door. It comes into my head. I don't know how, but I do not have to try. There's something in Eileen's voice as she reads, a tint, a tone that tugs. It takes me there. I'm transported. The words are hard, but I don't care because I get the gist. I listen because I want to.

I'm not asleep, but I could be dreaming. She's caught my attention. She has drawn me through my bedroom door. She has released me from my room.

I see the little man in the book, stomping in a hurry, trampling on a girl. He has no heart, with that ugly look of his. The girl has ringlets. She is a victim.

I'm so starved of colour that I feed on it in a frenzy, I gorge myself. It's like having another breakfast. I don't want her to stop. I'm hungry for more.

I watch Eileen's face and realise she is taken there as well, so I imagine us together, standing by that door, waiting for that man, wondering what to do.

Eileen would grab him too, collar him like Mr Utterson's friend, Mr Enfield, and make him pay his way. She is that kind of person, takes no nonsense. Am I the girl, trampled underfoot? Or do I help her catch him?

I study her lips, and marvel at their precision. She never makes mistakes, no stilted sounds like me. Every word is perfect. I know I cannot do this, but I want to try. She is putting on a show for me in a theatre of my own. We are watched by no one, except each other. No one judges us.

I like her accent, how it bends around the sounds, caresses them like living things. And it contains a strange reminder, a recognition.

I wish that Stan was here. I sense he would understand. I don't know why, it's just a feeling.

I realise. That's what Eileen is.

Eileen is a feeling.

*

'I want to take you to this place in the first chapter of The Strange Case of Dr Jekyll and Mr Hyde and to give it some atmosphere so that you feel like you are there. I want to paint a picture of the place where Mr Utterson and his friend Mr Richard Enfield walk past a door in a street which is somewhere in London that is very busy. It is posher than other estates because it is clean and shining like a fire in a forest and has freshly painted shutters which are things that go on top of windows in old houses, and a general cleanliness and gaiety, which ain't nothing to do with gay people but is an old-fashioned word for pretty. But there is a door of a building in this street which is not so nice, because the paint has more spots than my face and it does not have a doorbell neither. So this house ain't so posh, and so that's where the tramps sleep like the tramp who sleeps outside the Tesco Metro. This house

is sadder than the rest, you can just tell, and that is because inside is where the Mr Hyde who knocked the little girl down went to get money. He had a key. He was strange that man and so was the house. It was like that house and Mr Hyde both had the same personality. That house makes me think of me own house, which ain't happy neither. If the people inside a house are not nice or happy, then that is what the house feels like. I don't really know nothing about Mr Hyde, but he is why that house is scruffy and all the tramps want to sleep there, even though the tramp who sleeps outside the Tesco Metro does not seem unhappy. He says hello to me. Perhaps he thinks I'm another tramp, like him. I don't mind, he seems nice. Might be quite nice to be a tramp. Sometimes I feel like I'm a bit of a tramp in our house cause we ain't got stuff, like other people, I ain't blind. I'm just trying to be honest and all. I got to thinking about our house when I read about this house in the book, and I am glad I did. It makes you think, don't it, that maybe Mr Hyde ain't so happy after all because of that house. I mean, it ain't necessarily his fault, is it? Everyone hates him, but maybe it ain't his fault the way he is and all that. I just reckon we need to think about things like that because things ain't always the way they look. The end.'

*

I lie on the sofa and think about the book. The story is swirling in my head, making me dizzy. The people, the places, the aggro. It's almost like the entire world is living inside that book and it's spinning so fast it makes me sick, like I was sick on the bus when we went to Sheerness, that pukey mush that bubbles in your stomach, so deep it exists somewhere else, always about to rise up.

I need to slow this book down, grab hold of this planet by its handles and stop it from spinning. I must reach out and catch one of the people in it as they pass then clasp them so tightly it stops moving, like grabbing the railings of a playground roundabout that is turning too fast.

I reach for the first character to come to mind and, surprisingly, it's not any of the men who are the most important people in the story, but the little girl at the start. The girl who was trampled by Mr Hyde.

The writer does not describe her, but I picture Stella. My mother. As a child. She is blonde and tiny and running when My Hyde tramples her at the crossroads. She is the victim. I do not know why.

I'm very surprised by this thought, because it's the first time I've ever imagined Stella as a child. She's always been a drunkard in a dressing gown with fags for fingers. Not like a real person, who was once a child, more like a living disappointment, or a ghost that cannot be touched and never listens when you try to follow it through the wall.

And Stella is screaming on the ground, there in the street, tears streaking down her cheeks, her hair all messed up, her little arms and legs aching, her knees bleeding.

Then others gather round her and I realise for the first time that they know her and it is a surprise. The girl has a family. They are her parents, but they are hard to imagine. I just see a presence, forms like bodies, but the writer does not give them faces, and nor can I. They are dressed in that old-fashioned way and they mill around not knowing what to do and I want to tell them because I know the story. I want to help them.

They bend down and help the girl to her feet and rub the dirt away and hold her to them. They talk to her in soothing tones and check her arms and legs.

The story has slowed down now and I feel less sick. I can move the roundabout backwards and forwards to where I want. I can control the pace of what is happening.

I allow Mr Enfield to come across and take charge. He has seen what has happened and has collared Mr Hyde. He's in charge now and the girl stops crying. But he's not angry at Mr Hyde. He's angry at her mother, and I realise that she's no longer there. She's gone and I want her to come back. I rise from the scene and scour the nearby streets until I find her. She is sitting in a doorway like a tramp. She's drunk, but I feel sorry for her because I sense that she is ashamed.

I take her bottle and set it down and she looks at me. Now I see her face, and she is the spit of her daughter. I bring her back and make her rub away her daughter's tears. I give her a handkerchief to clean her cheeks. The girl is better now. I make her look at her mother and smile. Mr Enfield is no longer angry at her. He is angry at Mr Hyde, and I know that is the way the story should be.

24

*T*he *Strange case of Dr Jekyll and Mr Hyde* lies between us, closed, on the table. I've finished it. There's no one else here, but I can almost hear the applause.

I bet even your class at school haven't finished it yet.

I feel so proud of myself that I'm prepared to accept the compliment. Pride is like a warm meal filling me from within and leaving a powerful afterglow that gives me energy and contentment at the same time.

Ain't never finished a book before.

Eileen holds my hand. She senses this means a great deal to me and is surprised and heartened all at once. I imagine she is recalling the books she read at my age.

I think we should celebrate. How about I buy you a cup of coffee at Starbucks?

We go to the coffee shop and I have never been there, and we discuss *The Strange Case of Dr Jekyll and Mr Hyde*, about which I believe I'm now something of an expert, and I feel like an adult.

So what do you think was in that potion that he drank?

Probably brandy.

We laugh, although it wasn't meant to be a joke. Eileen seems to notice a double edge, but I change the subject.

I liked that book, miss. Can we read another one?

Of course.

What?

Well, we should read something a little bit more modern, don't you think? There's a book I think you will enjoy, it's a play for the theatre, a kind of murder mystery.

Eileen opens her bag. She has a new copy of the book ready and waiting. She places it in front of me like a gift.

Its title is An Inspector Calls. It's for the stage, which means there's a lot of talking, and that means you have to follow carefully what they say.

I nod. I am up for it.

They will be reading this one at school as well. Shall we try to beat them again?

I have the bit between my teeth.

But we also have to talk about the future.

What future?

Eileen sits back to signal that she is relaxed.

Well, Mrs Kavanagh says you need to do your GCSE like everyone else.

For the first time that morning, I bridle. My smile deserts me.

How do you feel about doing a GCSE? English?

I have to think. I look away, towards the window and the grey light of the rainy day.

I'm useless. Can't do a GCSE.

Eileen studies me. She seems to sense what I am feeling.

Mrs Kavanagh and I both think you can do it. Why not give it a go?

But what about, well, bunking off school? I ain't going back.

Eileen wants me to know that she is not making judgments.

I will still teach you.

I never expected to take exams. No one ever expected me to.

Don't have to tell Stella, do I?

*

I know she is waiting to pounce. A drunken cougar drying slowly in her dusty habitat, splayed across the savannah of the sofa. The room is as bare as blank paper. She will be using a cup as an ashtray but it will have already toppled and vomited a murky cocktail of cigarette butts and what might once have been brandy. This will soak into the weave of hair and ancient stains embedded in the pile.

Is that you?

Who else would it be?

I hear her shouting as I shut the door behind me. I know at once she's drunk. I enter and inspect her spread-eagled. A half empty bottle of brandy sits on a stain. That, too, will soon tip over like all the rest. It is only a matter of when.

Stella flicks ash across her outstretched legs.

Where was you?

Library. Tutor told me to go, din't she.

Stella waves her ciggie hand dismissively. Like the queen of bleedin England.

Library is it? Where's that then? Ain't this house good enough for posh Eileen?

Ain't posh.

Posh old cow, with all them papers.

Stella is trying to taunt me. It's second nature. There is something contrived about her cackle. I feel angry but do not rise to the bait. I'm used to being stalked.

'We was reading in the library.' She mocks me in an affected tone, pretending to be Eileen.

Hoi bleedin polloi. She jiggles her head to feign affectation.

Reading a book is ya?

Yeah.

Well you ain't reading nothing till you been to the chippy before Rob comes.

She pulls a crumpled ten pound note from her tight jeans and throws it at me. It bounces off my face and tumbles to the floor.

Useless cow.

I pick up the money and storm out. She gibbers in my wake, more grunts than language. On my way back, I nick some of Rob's chips. That's dinner.

*

Molly says you're teaching her Inglish. She already talks

bleedin Inglish.

I sit calmly, determined not to be lured by Stella's resentment into conflict.

English literature.

Stella purses her lips. A ripple passes through her shoulders, but she keeps her head still. This gives the impression of a puppet. She is being facetious. It is a small theatre, that kitchen, but it is nonetheless her stage.

Molly can't do that. She's useless.

Well, she's doing it.

Stella rests her elbow on the table and holds the burning cigarette vertical. The smoke conceals her face. She is hiding again. I can sense from her sideways glance that she is suspicious. She does not believe this yarn, spun to trap her, because she knows a thing or two about trapping.

I open my satchel and withdraw *The Strange Case of Dr Jekyll and Mr Hyde* and place it on the table, then push it forward.

She's already finished it.

Stella presses against the hard kitchen chair. A small tremor ripples through her falsely tanned arms. She looks down at the book, but does not touch it. Her eyes betray her.

Perhaps it is the eerie, superimposed faces of Arthur Batut's family on the cover to suggest the complex 'countenance' of a Victorian criminal that puts her ill at ease. She turns it over and places it down, cover first, so that there is no image leering at her, then pushes it back at me.

What's that about then? Looks rubbish.

It's in the curriculum. She'll be doing it for her GCSE.

No good to her. You need to teach her how to be less bleedin useless.

It will be a qualification.

I ain't got no qualifications, and I done all right.

There is no hint of irony in this comment. Stella shrugs and pulls on her cigarette. But she is uncomfortable.

Seems like a waste of time to me.

When we read the book together, Molly enjoyed it.

Stella chortles, but there is vulnerability in her laughter.
Well you ain't getting me to read no book with her.
She picks up the book again and this time flicks through it.
Not this rubbish, anyway.
She slaps the open pages with the back of her hand contemptuously.
I learn everything I need to know. The book is upside down.

25

Where do stories come from? Are they always there, in the head? Are people born with them like they are born with voices? Or do they just come out of the blue like an itch, caused by a movement, a comment, a smell? If that's the case, then why do some people get the itch and others don't? Why don't stories ever come to me? Why didn't they ever come to Stan?

I lie there at night thinking about this as I stare at the blank ceiling, the place I know best. I want to picture Stan, project him there with beams of light from my eye, but it's impossible. The dull white surface has such control over my mind that I can't make his face appear. All I see is his back, and he's walking out the door. Then it shuts.

I close my eyes to concentrate. I try to hear his voice, although he hardly ever spoke. It should not be difficult to imagine his voice, because it was so different, like no other I've ever heard. No one on the estate or at school spoke like that. But there is no sound either.

So there I am, unable to picture him or hear his voice. I feel weak. He's my dad but I can't see him. Surely I must be stronger than this, able to control my own head? Are the people who get the story itch only those who control their own heads? Is that why they have stories and I do not?

I decide to take control. I want to picture Stan because I miss him.

I start by trying to remember things that never happened. I begin with that strange body of his, skinny as an animal, not an ounce of fat. I roll up the sleeves of his sweatshirt, put the tattoos on his arm, give his fingers strength. I redden his neck because he's always outside. I stand him straight, his back strong. He seems proud to me.

Then I put him to work, and he's not doing the blackstuff or the bins but fixing the toilet in the bathroom. He's got a set of tools, spanners and the like, and he's whistling as he works. He's fixed the leak and we're all happy. Then he carries an armchair into the house and plonks it beside the sofa. He found it on a skip. He sits in it with a grin. God knows how, he's fixed the television.

Then I picture him at bedtime telling me a story.

I don't know why, but it's about a donkey. I like it. He sits on my bed and flicks through a book that we don't have, and my eyes are wide with wonder as he talks. Outside the night is young and the sky the dark blue of dusk just as it is before the streetlamps switch on. There are no clouds and the stars awaken.

All of a sudden, I can hear Stan's voice. It sounds like Eileen, strange but not unpleasant, and although the words are as unusual as those in *The Strange Case of Dr Jekyll and Mr Hyde* I can understand them and don't have to ask.

It's dark now and he's finished. I'm about to fall sleep but, at last, I can see his face. His eyes stretch with a smile that is the right way up, and his ruddy cheeks glow.

But as I drift off I wonder where this story came from. Did Stan find it in his mind or in a skip? This eats into my mind as sleep steals me away and in a final dreamy realisation I understand that none of this is real. I am remembering things that never happened.

Stan never told me bedtime stories. He doesn't have any.

26

He wants to tell Molly stories at bedtime, just like his da. Stan can picture this memory as he sits alone in his caravan in Whitstable, because the low light, the peaceful darkness of the site, is just the same. The silence is disturbed only by the bark of a dog or hoot of an owl in the fields yonder.

When his da told those stories, the boys sat against the pillows that they shared, three in a bed, two with minds and fists, and one nowhere at all. Stan has forgotten their names. The oldest was handy with the shovel but liked the sauce. He had no patience. He called Stan 'eejit' and kicked him like a donkey, then realised it was pointless. The middle boy was good with numbers. Their da took him to the horses and he helped Stan learn to read. It was slow going.

Their da told stories about old fiddler men, a fairy woman, and finding treasure in the soil. He spoke of a world neither here nor there, behind the real things that could be seen, a shadowland of simple truths. He peeled away the day to reveal what was beneath.

They were magic those stories, but to Stan the telling of them was more magical than what was told, because he remembered nothing. It was his da's voice, It was everywhere. A landscape. Stan liked his father's breathing, the clipped little words that he used which no one ever learned the meaning of, the snap of his anger when he lost his temper because that was real, the promise in his threats to smash faces like porcelain.

Yet no matter how hard he tries, Stan cannot remember what happened in the stories.

Details slip through the fingers of his mind like water. Little instants, objects that bring enchantment to life. His da told the same tales a hundred times, but kept the boys' attention nonetheless with the cadence of a familiar dream.

Stan tries to force himself to remember, as if digging out the soil for ballast on a driveway before it is compressed. This gives him a headache and he has to stop in case his skull caves in.

The only story he remembers fragments of was in the only book he ever read. It was in the caravan and survived his brothers, covered in crayon, frayed and thumbed to exhaustion. It was the story of the little donkey that carried Jesus.

Stan read that book a hundred times. He pressed his father to tell him the story over and over again even when his brothers stared in disbelief. What could be done?

He wanted to tell Molly about the donkey in the field near the site where the teacher called him special. He loved that donkey. Yet try as he might, he cannot remember the story about the donkey in the book. He left the gate in his head open and it wandered from the field. He is sad.

He pictures himself sitting on Molly's bed telling her the story, remembering everything then switching off the lamp to watch her travel into sleep.

He thinks of all of these things as he sits alone in Whitstable with only the stars, the crashing of the sea, a dog howling.

27

Finbar coughed blood as a child, but his da said it was the smoke from the turf that tickled his lungs and he'd be right as rain with a bowl of stew and a glass of porter.

He pictures the steam rising from the plate and the tin spoon he clutches. His father tugs the stopper from the stout and pours it into a little cup with giant hands chanting, *'Good man, good man, good man',* until his voice fades and so does he.

Finbar's eyes flicker. They open and shut. He is aware of the grey light of day through the window because the curtains have been opened but he cannot make out the frame because his eyesight is playing up. It is bright and he knows he has been here before, in that very same place, the brattle of his cough in an empty room, spitting bloody sputum into a wash bowl that his mother placed on the floor, unable to eat even though he normally has the hunger of a horse.

For an instant, that grey light takes him back again, and he no longer knows if he is six or seven but does know that his mother is concerned and puts extra blankets on the bed and when his father is in the field she carries him down and sits him by the range.

The covers are heavy on his body, and he does not have the energy to push against them. His arms are stripped of muscle, his face gaunt, the hide stretched tight across his cheekbones above hollow pits like pockets. He is so tired he cannot move, his long body extending the length of the bed. Breathless, his lungs scream for air, but he dare not breathe because it will start him off again and he cannot bear the weight of coughing. As a boy, he was pinned to the soil when the cart tipped and the ricks toppled, too weak to push them off. The breath would have left him then if the dog had not sensed his pain and fetched his father.

He hears footsteps on the landing. Someone has been

coming in and out and he thinks it is his mother but he can no longer remember what she looks like, although she says she is praying for him so it must be her. He thinks she is at the door but he drips with the fever, almost swims in his sweat, and does not want her to see him shivering.

He remembers someone else, a special friend who loves him, and they are in the field. She laughs at what he says and when she hits him playfully it does not hurt his shoulder because she is just a sprite and he cannot understand why he towers over her like a giant.

He sees her face and wants her to stay, but the grey light grows yellow and bright.

It swallows her up.

*

The moment of death was unseen. There was no need for Niamh to monitor his last gasps, take note of the quivering rattle as he struggled. God would do that. We come into this world alone, and thus we leave it. It was a formality. He had gone already. There was resignation in her bitterness, because this is the way it had always been.

As she sits rigidly at the kitchen table, her mind becomes disordered, cleaved from her as if not her own. She pictures the scene upstairs, the sunlight on the dingy windows, the washing bowl in which he will shave no more, the untidy bedclothes concealing his emaciated form, his pallid face sticking from beneath the bedspread, eyes wide with realisation, an outstretched bone. Suffering is divine, is it not? For those who have nothing to give, it is their offering. Finbar is experiencing a blessed truth.

She is already sketching out what lies ahead, still trying to solve the riddle of unhappiness perplexing her. A retreating farm with plundered land, no cow, hungry neighbours, and an insolent child whom she does not understand. The heavy weight of it all.

Time offers no consolation. Her grey eyes with pinhole pupils betraying loveless neutrality flit across the austere room. Is this it?

Her father had a herd, the best of the cattle the others said. She eased her solitude as a child in the dairy, washing the floor, brushing the water into the drain, turning the buckets on the slate.

She has sent Eileen to the field to dig potatoes. She will soon be back to disturb the peace, fretting about her father, forming questions a child has no right to ask. Spoiled, with an appetite for the attention of a man who failed them both. *'Let him die in peace, girl. He'll no more be here to coddle you, now, with his foolishness just to keep you amused. You'll learn the lesson that we all have to. Life is hard. Suffering is a blessed truth.'*

Niamh looks at the tray in front of her on the table, the tea cold in the cup, the bun untouched, sugary crumbs scattered across the plate, and thinks she hears more gasping.

28

Stella hovers. She is a ghost, haunting an empty home. I hear her fidgeting upstairs. God knows what she is doing. Never does nothing. Has nothing to do.

I have never listened to her from downstairs like this. Come to think of it, I have never sat here alone in the front room and listened to the house like this before. I can hear sounds outside on the estate. It is night, but someone shouts. A front door shuts, a car door slams, an engine starts. Then there is silence again. Now a screech, but it is not a person. A fox perhaps. I would like to know.

I sit here in the dark and enjoy myself. Something is unwinding. Thoughts are coming into my head. I have closed the door and I sit alone. I am glad it is not my bedroom. I will sleep here tonight, on this dirty sofa. I will bring down my pillow and sheet. I do not want to go upstairs, back to my room, to shut the door behind me. Stella will not know I am here.

I lie down on the sofa.

The television has a hole in it. The shelves are bare. There are dead flies on the window ledge. Light from a streetlamp filters through the dirty panes and casts flashing shadows on the wall. I reckon it must be windy because I sense a draught. Cool air puffs slightly against my cheeks. I like this sensation. I smile. Tomorrow, I shall walk outside.

I hear the bathroom door shut. She's in a bad mood, needs a drink, needs a fag, has no money. Rob has not been here for days.

I hear the floorboards creaking beneath her troubled weight as she paces to and fro like a caged beast. Her bedroom door clicks shut again. More creaking, more fidgeting. Thuds.

I think of Stan. I wonder where he is, who he is. I wonder if he is wondering about me. I know that he is alone with his strange mind and words. I wonder if he feels alone.

The fidgeting stops upstairs. The bed creaks. She is lying

down. She will fall asleep. She always does. It is all she does.

I cannot help her, and do not want to. The smell of brandy makes me retch. It wraps her like skin. She does not notice. Stan did not drink, so she drank for both of them. He did not talk, so she talked for both of them.

I have the strangest thought. I wonder if she dreams.

*

I want to use my new skill. Ever since Eileen asked me to describe what I had read, I have wanted to do this. Now I need to.

So I picture Stan reading a book, not kicking in a television screen, although that image flickers briefly like the final speck of light when a television is switched off. Coincidentally, he is reading *The Strange Case of Dr Jekyll and Mr Hyde*.

I know that this is fiction. He does not read books, but it warms me, nonetheless, the thought of him there, quiet, beside me. He looks up and smiles, that broad, sweet, charming smile.

There is a man in the children's section of the library sitting cross-legged with his daughter. He reads her a pop-up book slowly, pointing to the pictures. He checks her face with care to see that she is paying attention. I feel his love from the other side of the room. She is like a moth vibrating beside a light. She stares at him, fixed. She cannot move, the story has swallowed her like a whale.

I look at the book I am reading, and I know that there are more words on one single page than Stan has ever spoken to me.

I want to use my new skill. I recall once running to the upstairs window to watch the bin men coming down the street, waiting to see Stan just in his sweatshirt in the middle of winter, his strong arms and proficient strides, hoping he might look at me. I picture Stan looking at me the way the man in the library looks at his daughter.

I want to use my new skill. I remember the caravan on the

Isle of Sheppey when Stella spent the whole week drunk and Stan lost it. The dog ran away. But before that happened there was one night when we sat and looked at the sky. He was staring at it like the child looking at the pop-up book, swallowed up.

I want to use my new skill. I want to describe what I felt the last time Stan walked out. I felt despair, deep within my belly, misery. I thought at that moment something would pull me into the ground, some unseen, invisible force that cannot be resisted. I want to know what the word for this is.

I also felt a loss, but the kind of loss a person feels when something is broken, not as if it had been there in the first place and is now misplaced. A kind of regret. I also want to know what the word for this is.

29

L iam presses his hands together in prayer then points them down towards the surface of the water in the quarry. He extends his arms, looks back at Stella one last time, and smiles sweetly. A lifetime is contained in that smile.

One, two, tree ...

Then he is gone. Stella shuts her eyes and does not see him tipping himself over the edge and falling, falling, but she hears a faint splash when he hits the surface. She runs to the brink to look and cheer as she must, but holds back because this height poses a strange, magnetic threat. He is a brave boy, for sure. She sure is proud of our Liam.

She flattens herself on her belly and crawls to peer over, feeling the sharp little stones against her stomach, fearing the height will pull her after him. The water is black then green, a shadow disturbed only by the speckles of light on the tips of small waves that skip deceptively across it. She imagines how cold it will be and how she would flounder if it were her because she cannot swim. He is not there.

She waits for him to surface. She waits.

Then she shouts.

Liam?

She waits.

Don't be silly!

Nothing.

Are'dnt you holding your breath now, Liam?

The heartless ripples are nonchalant. A cloud casts an even darker stain over the reservoir. All she hears is the lap of a satisfied swell.

Nothing.

She waits, and it becomes forever. She plants her eyes on the flat rocks that splay out at the bottom of the outcrop then stretch beneath the surface until they melt and are lost in the darkness to see if he has crawled out, because he is always ribbing her for the sake of it.

Liam does not come up. The day is over when she gets back to the caravan. He has finally broken the family's weakened heart.

30

Something strange is happening to me. Part of me wants to imagine my mother in a classroom reading a book. Yet part of me does not want to think about her at all because she's not worth the attention. My mind insists on trying, no matter how hard it also resists doing so.

However, I can't imagine this. I've been been able to paint a picture of the road in which Mr Utterson and Mr Enfield first discuss the house of Mr Hyde. Yet no matter how hard I push down on my imagination, wring it like wet knickers, I just can't form a picture of my mother sitting in a classroom.

Finally, it comes to me in a dream.

She's holding a book but she's not reading it. Coincidentally, it's *The Strange Case of Dr Jekyll and Mr Hyde*, and it's the very same copy that I have been reading because hundreds of words that I do not understand have been underlined. But she's just holding it, not reading it.

However, Stella is not in a classroom. She sits at a school desk in the middle of a field. Behind her, by the gate, hunch a huddle of uneven caravans and the rusting red cadavers of burned-out cars.

Other children play on the wreck of a car without doors, jumping on its battered roof. They spit untamed shouts at her from afar, *'Join us, join us'*.

Stella wants to join them but she can't. She's being punished and is not allowed to move. She's not a child, but nor an adult. She smokes a fag and ignores a woman in a pinafore, holding a grubby baby without a face, screaming at her from the window of a caravan across the clod.

'Little scrubber.'

The children chant.

'Scrubber, scrubber.'

The woman puts down the baby and leans from the window as far as she can.

'No daughter of mine ...'

And the children chant.

'Scrubber, scrubber.'

'Wait till your da hears what you've been up to.'

Stella raises her eyes. Her looped earrings glint in the light bouncing from the open land. She pulls hard on her cigarette and tosses the butt to the soil.

31

When her father became sick, Eileen promised him she would do the reading, and she wanted nothing more than to sit at his bedside, but her mother would not allow it.

'He needs his rest. He'll soon be back in the field.'

The bouts of coughing that disturbed the night said otherwise. When all was said and done, death came with the speed of mercy, not from drowning in the rivers of green phlegm rising from the limestone substrate of his chest carved from the basin of north Kerry, or the shivering sweat off the sea from Ballyheigue, but from the delicate candle of his heart. It was spent of wax and one day extinguished. A wisp of smoke rose to be carried away by a breeze.

'Níl sa saol ach gaoth agus toit.'

What Eileen remembered most from that afternoon was the jarring voice of her mother announcing this rite of passage when she returned from the field. Diplomatic relations with God's consul displaced compassion for a child.

'He's gone. Fetch Father Hanlon, girl. Don't dawdle.'

That walk along the lane to St. Bridget's was the loneliest of her life, with no one out and just the stretching of the sky to remind her that this was not a childish dream and that life was, indeed, empty.

'Ma says da's gone, Father, would you be coming now?'

There were no hugs in the Murtagh household.

32

I'm in Stella's dream, and I'm surprised.

I was in the library with Eileen, and then suddenly I was here. I don't know how I got here. And I didn't know that Stella dreams.

It turns out that she does, but this is no expanding dreamland of elongated shadows and melting colours where people daub futures that they desire. It's a place of memories in which clocks tick backwards and the land shrinks, pulling Stella with it inwards towards a point in time and space that cannot be determined.

She is dragged by a force she can't resist through towns and suburbs and across forests and fields in constant motion, rotating like a weather vane, blown to and fro, a mote twisting violently in a storm.

I can't see her face, but then I understand what is happening. A vast tornado in the distance rumbles closer, across a muddy paddock, as I stand behind her back and watch, and I realise it's the twister and Stella that are still and the world that's spinning.

I'm giddy and reach out to clutch her, but she's too far to touch, and still I can't see her face.

Then it stops, a photograph. All around is still. And in the distance beneath the darkened sky, a caravan decorated with the silhouettes of two lonely figures who go about their business. Nally old, they are, and blind, with crooked backs they cannot straighten, and as I try to reach for Stella she tries to reach for them. She is too far across the field and her hand disturbs the scene with a catastrophic smudge that cuts in two this strange, unpainted world, and the caravan is gone.

Stella freezes. I can't see her face, but she's looking at her hand and seems confused. She doesn't know what she's done.

The world begins to twist again, and clumps of soil are turned into words that whirl around as it draws them into its voracious maw.

I remember it's a dream. It's Stella's dream.

She turns, but not to me, and at last I see her face. She's young again, but with a countenance of horror. She weeps.

Suddenly, I'm back in the library.

33

Stella stares at the mountain in the sink, but that is not what she sees. She sees a policeman crouching, stern, exasperated. He looms over a little girl who can smell the dank wool of his jacket. It has the odour of an animal. She hates this man. It is the same man who swaggered up to the caravan and told them to leave, called them thieving pikeys.

He points at the sign by the quarry.

'See that sign?'

Stella pictures herself, wagging her head, her little mouth gripped in childish obstinacy, denying everything, even reality, as she has learned how to do. She sees the sign but hates this man and will never help him.

'That says 'No swimming', doesn't it?'

She turns away, about to cry, so he grabs her by the chin. He does not care that her mother is watching. He does what he likes with his cruel power.

'Look at me when I'm talking to you.'

She summons as much defiance as she can, which is a lot for a child a fraction of his size, and stares at him with a beam of resistance that even he can detect.

'So why did he go in?'

Even at that young age she can perceive the lack of compassion in this man, the sense of relief that he would soon be rid of this family. She is too tiny to assemble the argument that had she gone to the school of the people who hate her she would have learned how to read the sign, even though the school can't teach them nottin'.

Her fists clench. Her fingers grow numb because she has squeezed all the blood out of them. She is angry at the man, angry at the people who do not travel and live in mushrooms and never swim in quarries. For the first time in her life she realises that she is angry at herself.

It is as if at this moment Stella becomes self-aware, realises she is here, in the here and now, alive, living and breathing and able to drown. Like Liam.

Two ambulance men pass them carrying a stretcher. On it is thrown a red blanket, creased. Liam is hiding under it, making himself flat like he does in the caravan to hide from his angry ma. As flat as death.

She expects him to burst out laughing. She wants to climb in there with him and have him tickle her, but the door of the ambulance slams shut and it is gone. They do not bother with the siren.

His mother is broken into pieces, so shattered she cannot be repaired. She kneels on the stony ground of the outcrop looking at the unforgiving volume of dark water in the cold night, sobbing mournfully into cupped hands, drowning in her tears for the naughty boy who drowned in the quarry.

After that, the very look of words wound Stella. The sign, the sign.

'See that sign?'

These words shout in her face that she had let her brother die. It was her fault. She had not read the sign.

'Look at me when I'm talking to you.'

Stella does not read, because she does not want to read.

III

1

*T*his is Bridie.

I look at the floor. I want the ground to open up and swallow me. I had this feeling on my first day at Calton High. A sense of impending doom. I am stupid. Useless. It will all go wrong. This girl will end up hating me. They always do.

I don't know what to do or say, but half nod a curt greeting. For Eileen's sake.

Bridie nods back. She's waiting in the classroom alone, the din of the arrivals at the Mudlark centre having died down and the corridor outside now silent. The atmosphere is calm, and I should not feel the sense of panic that I felt at school. The walls should not cave in.

To stop them doing so, I try hard to focus. I take note of Bridie's hair, but don't show this. It's immaculate, plaited at the sides, stitched in precise spirals against her head. The light shines on the glossy blue-black surface. Her fringe is gelled. Not a hair is out of place.

Bridie wears a dark business suit, skirt and jacket, buttoned at the front, and beneath that a pink blouse, pressed crisply. She smells of peach soap and her gold earrings dangle lazily from her earlobes, swaying with slow confidence like a boat bobbing on a ripple. She wears a clump of gold rings and her nails are filed to neat curves. Her shoes shine beneath the desk. She has folded one foot across the other with picture perfect poise. She is spotless. I am intimidated. I hope she is not like Bianca. She was spotless, too.

Eileen gestures for me to sit down, and I slide sheepishly into place. I cannot help noticing flecks of fluff on my dirty sweater, and look down at my scruffy trainers. There is mud on them.

Bridie is also doing her GCSE.

The girl smiles politely. She's business-like, serious. She

has placed an electric purple metal pencil case on the desktop and aligned this with its straight edge. I think she wants to be here.

Molly has read The Strange Case of Dr Jekyll and Mr Hyde already, Bridie, and is now on An Inspector Calls.

Bridie is impressed. Her eyes widen, and she flicks her head in recognition. Eileen moves to the door.

I have to get something from the office, I'll be straight back. You two wait here.

The door closes with a mild click. As I watch Eileen disappear, I notice that she takes a moment to glance back at us. We sit in nervous silence.

*

My first day at Calton High. It's like a brand, seared into my memory. A scar from a bad accident on a rainy day.

Stella was asleep and would not wake up. I didn't know where the school was and walked in the rain in endless circles. When I found it, the playground was empty and I knew that this was not right.

I waited at the gate. I zipped my anorak to the top because I was cold. I counted cars. I watched distant figures moving through the windows inside, where it was dry. I smelled the cooking in the canteen. I wanted to go to the toilet.

A woman saw me from a window in the school. She came out and walked across the playground carrying an umbrella. She had blue glasses and wouldn't smile. She seemed busy and bothered. I turned to run, but she called me, and I waited. She asked me what I was doing and I told her. I was waiting to go in. She scolded me and asked me where my uniform was. I told her I didn't have one.

She took me inside and said my mother must send me to school in a uniform. I asked her where to get one. I didn't want to tell Stella because I knew she would kick off and turn up at the school herself. There would be hell to pay. It would start worse than it already had.

The woman studied me. I could tell that she was trying to read my face. Then she told me not to worry. She would sort it out. She asked me where I lived. I could not remember. She looked me up on a list.

I followed her through the silent corridors. Our steps echoed on the polished floor. I sensed the height of the ceilings. My socks were wet and I felt them squelching as I walked.

We stopped at a red door and went in. The classroom was full of children and they fell to soft whispers when we entered. They watched me. I could feel their tongues.

The teacher was a man with greasy hair. He did not smile and later I discovered that he could not smile. His cheeks stuck out like ice-cream cones. He looked right through me and saw the door behind.

The woman spoke with the teacher and he nodded as if he didn't care. The other children watched him, waiting for their moment. They turned to me. They wanted to know what was being discussed.

The woman left and the teacher sat me at the back. He told another girl to help me. She gave me a piece of paper and said they were drawing.

'Draw a house. Draw your house.'

I did not have a pencil, so I left it blank. I watched the others drawing. They seemed to know what to draw. When the teacher came round to collect the sheets, he delayed beside my desk. It was as if he did not understand. How was it possible that this child cannot draw a house. I knew what he was thinking. I wanted to speak, to issue a lame excuse.

'I don't have a pencil.'

But as I pushed the muscles of my mouth to move, the bell rang and he sent us out. The others ran into the playground and so I followed. They gathered around in clumps and pointed at the girl without a uniform. They whispered. Someone pushed me into the boys' toilets and held the door shut.

*

Bridie turns to me.

So what you here for?

I'm surprised by how quickly she has spoken to me, taken an interest. It's not normal. I don't know how to respond. I stare at the desktop.

There is silence again. Bridie crosses her tidy hands on the desk and looks out of the window. I realise that she's being patient. So I talk.

We was working at the library. Eileen brought me to have a look. See if I want to come.

She turns in her seat to face me.

It's all right here. She's all right, Eileen. No stress.

I nod timidly. As if anyone cares. Bridie looks at my dirty, flecked jumper that sags from my shoulders like a Mrs Nally bag of lumps and scans my faded jeans and trainers.

She swings her legs and swivels in her chair towards me. I notice that she is smiling. I sway between feeling at ease and feeling suspicious. Bridie has a mouth on her.

Just so's you know, I'm disruptive.

A vast smile breaks across her face. It glows, like sunrise.

Talking back. At teachers. They got fed up with me, so I was excluded. Course, don't talk back at Eileen. She don't care anyway. She can talk back at anyone, so there's no point.

There is another silence but I feel my body opening up and my face signalling that I'm listening, relaxing. Bridie continues. She certainly likes talking.

So what you here for? Must have done something. Everyone here's done something.

She guffaws and it catches me by surprise and I like it. I grin and answer.

Bunking off.

Bridie lowers her head and voice, almost imperceptibly, conspiratorially, as if plotting. Two convicts in a cell.

Go girl!

I don't know what that means. But it sounds good. There is more silence. I don't know what to add. Bridie talks.

Nice and quiet here. You'll get your GCSE done all right, I reckon. No bother.

I know I must give something back. She is making an effort. I gesture at her plaits.

Like your hair.

Her face lights up. It was the right thing to say. I feel elated. I've done something right.

Thanks. My mum done it. Spent ages.

Bridie gestures at my stinking sweater. I know it is gross, but it is all I have.

Think that's Kashmir. Can make it look a lot better if you roll up the sleeves. Here.

She reaches over and I flinch. I want to move back, fall off my chair, run from this room. But she is too fast and before I know it she has pulled out my arm and is rolling my sleeve as if it were a sausage until it curves back up the forearm like a doughnut. I feel the touch of her hand. Another human being. I am almost overcome.

She smiles at me. I realise she is being kind. So this is what it feels like. Then she pulls the other arm out and does the same. It is intoxicating. She sits back and admires what she has done.

That's better.

2

The boneyard at Duagh is covered in a mist as eternal as death itself. Droplets of water cling to cracked vases and lockets of hair draped upon Celtic crosses. Wilting dahlias sag from old milk bottles. Brambles enmesh unkempt plots. It is a graveyard. It is meant to be a miserable place.

Niamh Murtagh, widow, mother of Eileen, housekeeper to Father Seamus Hanlon, does not need a graveyard in which to exercise her miserable vocation, but rises to the occasion nonetheless. She stands beside the grave dressed in the black she has been saving beneath a green umbrella held by her dutiful daughter. She watches the priest with stern attention. He chants an oration as he commits a crude casket to a bed of clay.

... sleep here in peace until you awaken him to glory, for you are the resurrection ...

No hands are held, embraces conceded, or smiles of resignation proffered at the passing of Finbar Murtagh, farmer, late of the parish of St Bridget's, a big man whose even bigger mortal limitations weigh heavily upon the shoulders of his widow.

Amen.

The other mourners are mostly wizened women from the church for whom attending funerals is the weekly hurling match. No bank clerks or shop men here. Some neighbours have come to pay their respects with their florid faces and stitched cheeks battered by the open air. The widow shakes their hands coldly to a dirge.

Sorry for your loss ...

The priest leaves. They are alone.

Eileen looks at her mother's face. She is trying to discern what the woman is feeling, if she is feeling anything at all. She realises that her mother is the same, has not changed. Worse, her life with him had been an entire preparation for widowhood.

This is a consummation.

The arrangements had been made from memory, with little attention to the detail of the man, but devotion to timeless rites. There had been a wake, but widow Murtagh pronounced that it would be dry and so the few old fellows who turned up took off their hats, crossed themselves reflexively by the coffin on the kitchen table, took note of the open window, then left for O'Brady's and the dark stuff to get the oppressive smell of that woman out of their Sunday best.

Across the cemetery, Eileen notices the gravedigger leaning on his shovel, waiting patiently for them to leave. He catches her eye and tips his cap, as if to remind her that he has a job to do and it is merely a matter of saying their goodbyes so he can get on with it and then back down to O'Brady's himself with the rest of them to discuss the price of butter beneath pictures of boxers and jockeys.

Eileen studies her mother's expression as she looks down at the casket in its sodden hole with blank relief that this job is now done, at least. He is gone, but it makes no odds because it is too late to change her lot.

She turns, oblivious to her daughter, who hears her muttering as she tramps away from the hole to the path.

At least he wore his suit.

The girl remains there, numb. She seeks to wring out as much pain as she can so that it does not stay with her like an infection. The thought of being left alone with her mother overwhelms her.

*

The other room has become a cold enclosure, taken possession of by her mother. Off limits. The woman disappears after dinner every night, to be neither seen nor heard thenceforth. She insists on reading the *Holy Lives of the Saints* to the exclusion of all else. She adds the word '*Holy*' to its title even though Eileen knows this is not what it is called.

'I'm in the other room, now. Don't be disturbing me.'

Eileen finds her own bibliography at Abbeyfeale library. She cycles there as often as she can, a refuge in the shelves from her ascetic reality.

But her mother is not happy. Arms folded, she stands in the kitchen doorway waiting for her to return to do the last chores of the day. She will hear no excuses. She berates her before she is even off her bicycle.

'I don't care if you were reading the Holy Bible. God hates indolence.'

Chores mean the housekeeping that her mother cannot do because her ghostly presence possesses the priest's house, which she cleans for free. Endless hours polishing in the name of the Lord for not even a loaf of bread infuse her with the odour of Brasso and altar wine, and not even from drinking it.

That privilege is left to Father Hanlon, who for all his piety props up the bar at O'Brady's and accounts for much of its income. This is no whiskey priest. This is a porter priest. The 'Heavenly Chit', O'Brady calls the man's lengthy tab.

Eileen knows this to be so because her father told her.

3

Stella lies in bed waiting. Rob is done for, and she is miserable. He has form. He has been nicked. He does not usually make mistakes, but has slipped up.

The police turn up to search her house, show who is boss. It does not take long, because there is nothing there anyway. She complains bitterly nonetheless, cackling on. They have heard it all before. They ignore her like a mosquito.

'He's going down.'

Stella slumps in the kitchen after they have gone and pulls on those drooping cigarettes. They found a bazaar of electrical equipment, microwaves, televisions, even toasters in the lockup. They pinned a dozen jobs on him. Old Bill is cock-a-hoop.

Stupid.

Stella mumbles miserably as she sits there, eyeliner staining her face. She has been trying to avoid thinking about what has happened so she does not have to confront reality. The thought of being alone again.

She pictures Rob languishing in jail. He is with his mates, having a whale of a time. He smokes on his bunk, sits in the canteen eating chips, chats inconsequentially about doing bird and football. She is alone.

She likes his chirpy, carefree manner. His smooth face and meatless body, the way he plays pool at The Saddle, the effortlessness with which he glides.

She likes the tattoos he is collecting on his arms and neck like walking graffiti, pointless whorls and smudges, some of which are in Chinese, although she knows Rob cannot talk Chinese because no one can talk Chinese.

She does not taunt him. But there is no sense that she is meant to be with him, no depth or complexity to this liaison. It is transient, whatever it is, always on borrowed time. Rob knows this too. She is twice his age.

She stares at the muddy footprints left by the police on the kitchen floor and pulls on her cigarette then exhales into the cold air.

Then she thinks of Stan.

Stan never nicked nothing, even though the Callaghans he worked for did cars at night after laying roads. He was stupid, but never stole nothing, and therefore not stupid enough to get caught. Jesus taught him that. His brothers didn't listen.

Suddenly, the thought of Stan makes Stella smile. It comes upon her unexpectedly and evokes a surprising sensation that confuses her. She indulges herself exploring it, this other side to her character. It is affection. It is fleeting, but there nevertheless. Unmistakable.

Stan did what he was told. But he could not drive and did not tell the Callaghans until it was almost too late. So they left him standing there.

'Useless eejit.'

It was why he stuck to laying driveways, which was a great relief because he really did not want to steal. What would the donkey think?

Stella is strangely relieved. This relief is also a surprise to her.

She fights against admitting it, but does not mind that Stan just stuck to driveways. She will miss Rob and his cash, but driveways are grounded. You cannot steal them. They outlive you.

And, it also had to be said, Stan was good at driveways. He seemed to understand them, if that is possible. She had watched him at work, followed his eye along the line of a border, calculating without knowing.

She pictures him crouching beside a layer of ballast, checking the level with his thumb. His sleeves are rolled up, and she takes in his hairy forearms. Something stirs. His forehead is furrowed with concentration. She sees his grey eyes flicker as he measures the gradient with a hidden algorithm that he never knew he knew. In the distance is a caravan park and sheer white cliffs beyond capped with a rolled mat of green as smooth as asphalt.

She stands there, beside him as he labours.

*

A tear rolls down her cheek. Stella does not wipe it away.

Eileen says nothing, but tries not to look into her eyes. She smells the dry, sickly odour of addiction on Stella's skin. It is time to talk.

Are you all right?

Stella now feels the tear on her cheek and wipes it away. She sniffs and inhales robustly.

Fine.

She pulls a ball of toilet paper from her pocket and wipes her nose, then blows it like an explosion. She reaches for her cigarette packet. It is empty.

Bleedin ...

She tosses it angrily across the kitchen. It hits the dirty dishes in the sink but Bowl Mountain is unmovable, and it bounces to the floor.

Eileen is generous in her compassion, even though she does not like this woman. She reaches across and touches Stella's hand. The skin is clammy, as if she is only half alive.

Do you want to talk about it?

Stella wipes her nose again.

Rob. He's going down for five years.

More tears.

All I got was a bleedin phone call.

Eileen now holds both of Stella's hands. She waits.

I ain't got a penny.

What about Molly's father?

Stan? Bleedin disappeared ...

Eileen clasps her tighter. Stella snorts. She attempts a clumsy restoration.

He was always away, but he's gone for good now.

Eileen listens. Stella wants to talk.

It was me. I ain't excusing nothing. He just got fed up.

Everyone does.

Her face screws up and she starts to weep. She presses it into her palms. Eileen moves her chair and puts her arm around Stella's back. The stench of alcohol is almost overbearing. Stella gestures towards the cigarette packet on the floor.

Need a fag.

Eileen nods.

Would you like me to bring you some?

Stella is revived.

Marlboro. Molly knows which.

*

Stella steals a bottle of brandy from the shop.

It is high on the top shelf, but Asif has left his steps by the freezer. Even though she is as short as a bad temper, she can reach it with the tips of her fingers.

She flicks it from the shelf and catches it like a baby thrown from a burning building then stuffs it in her sheepskin. She hops down to survey the cooked meats, all innocent like.

Unwittingly, Asif has created a blind spot. A bloke walked in with a cricket bat on a Sunday night and threatened his mother so he installed Perspex screens. They imprisoned him behind the counter.

Stella was born understanding blind spots. She curbed her enthusiasm for them when shirtless Rob came into her life, but still recognises them. She also knows that Asif never turns on the alarm because she has stolen from him before.

She spends the rest of the morning prising off the security tag. Nearly takes her eye out with a kitchen knife. A touching reminder of when she was young. She runs her finger across her cheek, along the edge of her jaw. She feels the sting of knuckles, but she does not remember whose they were. Her father. Her mother. Whoever.

She is alone in the house. This is unusual. Molly is at the library. Rob is awaiting trial.

He called her from the remand centre.

'Visit me.'

Stella promised, but lied. The idea of being locked away rattles her. It offends a wounded instinct, the freedom to leave anything anywhere at any time. Most of all, Stella wants to leave Stella.

She knows Molly dislikes Rob. With a vengeance. She knows he robbed her too, swiped a fiver from her bedroom. He can't help himself. It is an addiction.

She sits on her bed sipping neat brandy with relief, and now wishes she had stolen a bottle of Coke to go with it. Stealing Coke is harder. The bottles are bigger. Can't exactly flick them.

She looks around the bedroom at the grubby walls and empty shelves. Light filters in through thick grime on the windows. Her clothes lie in stinking piles on the floor. She has been unable to visit the laundrette for a lifetime. She is broke.

She pictures the caravan on the Isle of Sheppey. It was not as dreary as this. Caravans do not need to be filled with things. She did not take clothes with her, so she could not have left them on the floor.

Then she is gripped with longing, to be there, turn her back on this grim inactivity. In this place everything stands still and it is impossible to change yourself because the landscape never changes.

She takes another swig. The brandy is beginning to lose its taste. Coke would have sweetened it up, but could not sweeten up her life.

She tries to picture Rob in the canteen, or the exercise yard, his sleeves rolled up, a cigarette behind his ear. She has lost every man to have passed between her legs. She is developing a fear of mirrors.

Stella wants something better. She wants to do something, because she knows she can do nothing.

4

Eileen inspects her tea. It is the colour of dirt.

'Don't sip the mud.'

She looks up. His cheek is pure charm, and for a young nun fresh out of Ireland the Scouse lilt soothes in that dangerous urban sprawl.

Micheal. A voice that makes light of everything, floating above setbacks like the steam off smouldering turf, whispering to her as he would with his last breath that he was there, taking nothing seriously, he would always be there.

It is a rare instant when she is lost for words, her eyes drawn not to his but the slurry in her cup in the battered staffroom of St. Philomena's comprehensive, the best that deprived Bootle can offer.

When she does look up, she is swallowed by the sweet mischief of his smile, the flushed cheeks and humour in his gaze, the forlorn glory of his curly mop, as dark and wild as the Spanish Main.

He sits and introduces himself, betraying secrets to the girl from Duagh with unholy wit about each of her colleagues in the besieged room. The head, whose political connections stretch to the White House if you are to believe what you are told, the master of mathematics, who collects gravy on his tie then wrings it out at home, the geography teacher who cannot tie his shoelaces.

'They're a wild bunch when you get them down the pub. Talking of which ...'

He asks her where she is from, and knows it.

'My parents were from Tralee. I'm steeped in it, like tea.'

He asks her why she became a nun, quipping that it's a filthy habit, knowing that she will not care, and she does not.

He asks her where she's going with it, the religious life, and tells her why he's there. He talks about the city, and asks her what she thinks.

She is smitten. He bowls her over.

Eileen stares into her cup as she sits in the staffroom of the Mudlark centre. The tea is bitter now, but the memory a sweetness from long ago that she has not forgotten how to taste.

They had planned to visit Ireland, but were frustrated by circumstances, his sickness, the unexpected confusion.

Some people are not destined to live long, Eileen tells herself. They are spared disappointment and regret. They colour those around them with a hue of something that is not sadness and then are gone.

I loved you, she whispers.

She puts down her cup. Her patience is immense, a mastery of time. If only she could convince her body that it was being fooled, and that the stiffness in her arms and legs and cracking knuckles and diminishing eyesight were just deceit. Micheal taught her that. His absence is a deceit.

*

It was a vernacular interpretation, but had the same meaning. Eileen hears the voice of her father as they sit in the other room, him tapping his temple with a sausage of a finger.

'You can plant as much as you like, girl, but what matters is the harvest.'

To Eileen's mind, this was what Alfred North Whitehead is saying in the textbook she is studying, with those posh words of his.

'Valuable intellectual development is self-development.'

Micheal does not disagree. He drives her to the teacher training college then drives her home. She studies at night. He does not care whether she is a nun or not. He is carefree, so laid back he's horizontal. All he cares about is being with her.

She knows it will be impossible to remain living with the Sisters while living in sin. The Sisters laugh at that, and whisper to her that love is forgiveness. They are as excited for her as they are sad at her leaving. The ripple caused by Eileen

Murtagh is merely lost in bigger waves.

The couple move in together. It hums as a rumour at St. Philomena's school, but just for a day. The teachers are too busy holding back the deluge.

The two years they spend together are glorious. They are made for each other, an easy passion that floats without turbulence or direction.

Micheal would have married, but they never do and he falls sick and then it is too late. When he develops headaches, he is dismissive, self-deprecating. When he loses his balance and slurs his words, she knows it is serious. By the time he is diagnosed with a brain tumour, it is too late.

Their last month together is torture, then grief stops her in her tracks. A malevolence within convinces her she is to blame. It has the voice of her mother.

Aoife takes her arm and leads her away from the crematorium. Even in death Micheal was humorous.

'Put a match to me. I'll go out like a ciggie.'

She meets his family for the only time, but there is nothing to say. Grief also grips them in its claws.

Aoife takes her to the pub but the pain is obstinate. The children notice. They catch her weeping at a window. She sees whispers about lost love and the heavy weight of mourning swirling darkly from the mouths of colleagues.

Aoife takes her away. They fly like birds to Bermuda and a different school under a different sky.

Micheal follows her, but does not demand attention in his lonely residence. He nudges her gently to remember sweet talk and wit, kisses on the beach. And Eileen does, and grows strong again, if not whole.

Then one day she sees the children. They are sitting in anticipation for her to tell them about William Shakespeare and where Kenya is and why churches have copper wires on their steeples.

5

I feel the vibration of the car door shutting, jolting me back into the here and now. Eileen slides back into the driver's seat. She has taken cigarettes to Stella. I realise what she has done.

You don't have to buy her fags. She don't bleedin deserve it. I know I don't.

Eileen takes out her keys and sticks them in the ignition. There is an edge to her tone. It is interesting, and I try to sense its meaning. It is saying: '*I shall do what I want.*' I want to understand this. But that is not what comes out.

She'll be asking you for money next.

Well it's lucky I haven't got any, then.

Eileen starts the engine and the car pulls out. We weave though the estate like a thread of colour, a bright green car daring the grey concrete. She turns into the main road and joins the traffic. She remains silent, but I can tell what she is thinking. I have control of my mouth now, and because I respect what she has done and want to say thank you, I volunteer information about Stella.

It's the drinking.

Eileen says nothing, but expects more. I sense it.

Got really bad when Stan left.

Eileen appears to take the comment in her stride, as if I'd discussed the boozing with her before and it's well known between us. But I've hardly mentioned it and, to be honest, don't know why I'm doing so. It's as if one side of who I am is now speaking without asking the other for permission, but it's a side I think I like. It seems to be more serious, more grown up. So I let it continue, although I turn my face away to look out the passenger window at the passing streets. It is less of a distraction than trying to interpret Eileen's reaction.

Stan just got fed up with all the other blokes. Anyone bleedin would. Whole estate thinks she's a slapper. He belted her, then buggered off. Everyone knows.

I do not know where that came from. When I hear my own voice I realise that the choice of words sounds just like Stella. Am I a mini-Stella? Is that what the other side of who I am is? I hope not.

Eileen busies herself driving, and I am not certain she is listening. We stop at traffic lights. She turns to me.

Do you really think they know, Molly?

Of course they do. Although I admit I'm taken aback by her question.

Course. All the people at school know. Stan ... belted ... Stella.

Then, for reasons I don't understand, I feel the skin round my eyes tingling and tightening. Emotion rises but I've no idea where this comes from. I thought the serious side of me was now in control, but I start to cry, grateful for the fact that my face cannot be seen, although Eileen realises. And my voice continues even though I really want it to stop. I do not like this side of myself after all. It is too exposed.

Thing is, she ain't a bad person. She's got a mouth, but she ain't what they say.

I feel my face screw up into a ball of wrinkles and pain. It's uncontrollable. I'm confusing myself. I don't know why, but I'm defending Stella. I want the car to stop, to get out and walk. The sobbing convulses my body. My chest heaves. Eileen pulls over. I hear the indicator light clicking.

Is that why you stopped going to school, Molly?

I say nothing, but I snivel and that's enough. She touches my hand. And then my serious side kicks off in that bleedin voice again.

All talking about me, and me being useless and all, and Bianca, taking my knickers, and Mr Butler hating me ... couldn't stand it.

This could go on forever. Tears flood out like blood and I cannot staunch them. Eileen reaches into the glove compartment for a box of tissues. She hands it to me.

Do they really know?

Everyone knows. I mean you knew.

Eileen shakes her head.

I didn't.

I look at her studying my ugly mug streaked with tears. I'm numb with shock.

And if I didn't know, how could anyone else?

*

I want a book.

The woman who has marched to the counter of Roundwell library has wild, over-bleached hair and wide, manic eyes. She is looking around with shifty unpredictability like a scared animal, standing on tiptoes to see between gaps in the shelves, waving her head from side to side. She appears to be looking for someone. Or perhaps someone is looking for her.

The librarian confronting her is bewildered and tempted to reply with sarcasm, thinking this might be some kind of joke, to sweep her hand around imperiously as if to say, *'Look around, we are surrounded by books, take your pick',* but she does not. Instead, the librarian decides in a reflex that her best course of action is to humour this woman. She pushes her spectacles back up her long, straight nose and tips her angular head to one side. This is meant to be a gesture by which she signals professional interest in her subject, but it has never quite worked, and she has discovered that many of her customers find it irksome. Remembering this, she straightens her head immediately.

What kind of book are you looking for, madam?

Under normal circumstances, being called 'madam' would have pulled the pin of Stella's grenade. Crouch, put your hands in your ears, count down from ten, and close your eyes. But it does not. Stella is distracted, her furtive glances in every direction confirming that she is definitely looking for someone.

Any old book.

There it is again. The librarian is having trouble determining whether this woman is being serious. She coughs in an effort to concentrate and give herself a moment in which to decide the safest way to reply.

Fiction, non-fiction?

What?

A story?

Yeah, a story.

The librarian points to a shelf of popular fiction and Stella is off like a shot but is distracted by the children's section. She picks up the first book she finds and sits down at one of the tiny tables.

The librarian's eyes follow her. She has been at this branch on the Roundwell estate for several years now, and it is clear from this woman's voice that she is not a big reader. The people who come in are generally the same old crowd. A few old regulars who read the paper, parents with their offspring who inhabit the children's section, a few youths who drift in to do their homework, occasionally borrow a graphic novel. That's about it. Oh, and the lady from the Mudlark centre with her pupils. There is rarely a visitor like this woman, overcome with a sudden passion for reading.

Stella flicks through the book. Something about crocodiles by the look of the pictures. But she has positioned herself there because she has seen what she has come to see. She has seen Molly sitting with Eileen at the back. She has ventured in to observe them.

Strange, unnatural thoughts rampage through her head as she does so, ideas that she has never had before, hostile intent, jealousy.

Molly is talking to Eileen, and talking and talking. They are looking together at a book that Eileen is holding open, and Molly is smiling. They look so natural, as if they have been together forever.

For a brief instant, Stella is almost overcome with indignation, prompted to stand, fling her book about crocodiles to the floor, march across, grab Molly by the wrist and announce, *'That's my girl you're hogging! Mine, get it?'* but at that moment Stella catches from the side of her field of view the librarian watching her, and she feels exposed. She returns to her picture book, and flicks the pages with mock enthusiasm. The woman looks away.

The rage passes, and in its place leaves questions and doubts.

Stella asks herself why Molly talks to Eileen and never talks to her. Why she prefers someone she has only just met. What Eileen can give her that Stella cannot. Why she prefers someone who is not even her flesh and blood to her own mother.

When the answers to these questions come to her, they are as surprisingly simple as the images in the book about crocodiles. Something within her snaps, almost audibly, leaving her open-mouthed.

Stella drops her book and looks at her hands. They are the hands that held Molly as a newborn baby, but they are not the hands that are holding open a book for her now that she is no longer a child.

When the librarian looks up again, the wild woman is gone. There is a book about crocodiles on the floor.

6

I grumble and so does Bridie, but Eileen knows our protestations are half-hearted. We *want* to read out what we've written about *An Inspector Calls*. It is easier to do this when there is just the two of us. We give each other strength. Bridie coughs theatrically.

'First there is this bloke called Arthur and he's really posh and rich, and because he had loads of money he thinks he's the bees knees and is a bit of a know it all. Then there's his wife, Sybil, and she's a bit of a sheep, don't want to upset him or nothing. Might do well if that woman stuck up for herself a bit more. Then there's Sheila, the daughter, who's getting married and she's pretty, blonde, with nice skin, and curls down to her neck. And even though her dad told her she must marry this bloke she kind of fancies him anyway because he's quite fit, and he's rich as well, and she's never had a boyfriend.' That's it.

Eileen claps with appreciation.

Your turn Molly.

I adjust myself in my seat. Want to get this right. I'm nervous because although I have read to Eileen, I have never read in front of Bridie. I want to make a good impression. I catch Bridie's eye, I feel myself blushing.

'An Inspector Calls. Arthur is the father and he's very posh and because he's so rich he thinks he's the only piece of buttered bread on the plate and knows everything. His wife Sybil thinks so too, but as she don't want to wind him up she just agrees with him all the time. I reckon she's quite a small person, not very high, a bit of a weakling, while Arthur is probably really big and fat, like as if because there's loads of blubber there he can throw his weight around, you know. But I reckon that if you really pissed off Sybil she would snap back, cause just because she's little don't mean she's a pushover. Sheila is the daughter and is very excited because she's getting married and thinking of that bride's dress, like Jordan's dress,

you know, when she married Peter Andre, pink and fluffy. And her dad Arthur has said to her you can have any dress you like cause I got so much money it don't matter. And Sheila the daughter will look really great in that dress because she's pretty and she's done her hair. It ain't bleached but naturally blonde and she's got ringlets which always make you look good even when you're dead. She don't know the bloke she's going to marry that well, because, well, it don't matter in them rich families do it? But she likes him and he's all right, he ain't going to whack her or nothing. So she probably fancies him.' And that's it.

Eileen claps again. She keeps her hands together, thrilled at what we have given her.

The bell rings.

*

It's no bother. I've got a Saturday job. No worries.

The face that talks back at teachers and has seen Bridie chucked out of a string of schools melts into a sweet smile as we enter the coffee shop. I detect that smile's warmth, even though I'm screaming inside. I'm terrified of being exposed, ignorant of friendship, mired in the expectation that it is bound to end badly.

But Bridie has a sixth sense. She senses that I'm alone, in fear. Damaged goods.

Have you started your essay?

I nod.

At the counter, Bridie says I can have anything I want. Even cake. No one has ever bought me cake. I'm too shy to ask, so Bridie orders two pieces anyway.

I'm having trouble, Molly, to be honest.

Bridie takes the papers from her satchel, and reads out our assignment.

'What is your favourite character and why?' Thing is, I don't have a favourite.

Suddenly, there is that voice in my head again, the sensible one. I don't know where it comes from. It whispers in my ear. I repeat what it says.

Your favourite character should be Eva.

But she's dead.

Yeah, but that ain't got nothing to do with it, see, Eva worked in a shop, and so do you.

Bridie smiles.

What do I say?

Just go through and find out what it says about Eva, then write that down.

Bridie raises her hand for a palm slap. I don't know what this is, so instead she offers me the second piece of cake.

So who's your favourite?

I know now this is not a trap. It is a simple question. Bridie just wants to know. She is interested. There's no agenda. I take out my copy of *An Inspector Calls* and flick through it.

Eric.

Blimey, the soak?

I understand that this is an important moment.

I know all about soaks.

*

It is something to do with money. Cost cutting.

Eileen is trying to explain to us that we will be joining a bigger class, but I know she is lying. It's a white lie. A good lie. Bridie knows that too. Eileen would never hurt us.

We have other pupils, and so they think that if one teacher has a class of five or six, then they don't have to pay for two teachers with smaller groups, like you two. They just want to save money.

We complain, but Eileen can sense it is again half-hearted. To be honest, we've realised that as long as we're together, it doesn't matter.

And they are all in the same boat, they won't even notice

you're there. They'll be just as nervous as you are.

I look at Bridie.

Can we sit together?

Eileen laughs, but is not mocking.

Always.

The new class has boys. They have problems too, but they behave. They aren't like Rob. They want to do their GCSEs. Bridie fancies one of them. I can tell. She does something odd with her eyelids. We laugh about it.

It feels like school should feel.

7

Stan runs along an empty beach. His strong frame pushes into wet silt, pressing into the cold sand. Shingle lines the seafront and his tarry boots protect his feet from larger stones that litter the lower reaches, half buried. Grains cling to a twist of bitumen on a toecap.

He is lost, even though he knows exactly where he is. On the beach.

He knows the word for Stella's behaviour. It is anger, and always there. She gulps it from the air like it were a bottle that is always full. But his anger is not the same as hers, and he wrestles with this sense that there is something else. He does not know the word for this, and searches for a picture instead. But he feels its weight and wants to lift it like a wheelbarrow.

He wants to talk to her, but cannot. He wants to ask her questions, find out what's wrong, try to make it better. It is almost as if her bottles have messages in them. She drones on endlessly, but wants to say something else.

He stops and catches his breath. He cannot run for ever. His lungs burn like they do at work. A cough slaps his face. He sits and watches the gulls.

She never met his family. He tries to picture them again, his father in the pub, his brothers by the door, his mother in herself. They are becoming harder to remember now. No one smiles. They are angry. It was Coventry, where they lost him. A place he does remember. A car park. They just left.

He feels inside his pocket, and although it is empty he touches a roll of cash. Da gave it him and then was gone. Just like Stan has gone from Stella.

He slouched more, his da, with every passing day, the fight over. It was a hundred pound he gave him. He must have cared.

Stan sees him. His da's eyes beneath his cap are blurred but his pasted cheeks are not, a mesh of veins raked across translucent skin like an asphalt driveway. He touches Stan with his hand as he passes him the cash, his fingers the only part of him still strong, his jagged nails uncut. Stan feels that touch.

He wonders where those hands are now. Wrapped around an empty glass, just strong enough to lift it.

She would have wept, his ma. But she would not have spoken. She would have watched him walking back across the car park. She would have known. She had a sense, a way of seeing things, he never understood it. She would have sat as they drove away later that night, stared at the stars, and blinked to destroy a tear.

They would have laughed, his brothers. They would have quipped and scrapped with their tongues and told his da he was right to dump the *eejit*, then heaved themselves off to bed to dream about breakfast. They would have forgotten by now Stan was ever there.

Coventry. He will never go back.

Seagulls perch on a wall before returning to the sky. Stan thinks of Stella. It is so easy to lose someone if you are on the move.

He wants to shout, but cannot find the words.

8

A oife told me. She leant forward over the table, eyes wide as moons, intense with their burden.

'Father Hanlon went to the farm.'

Her cheeks blushed. It was hot in the pub, and it could have been the whiskey, but I knew it was something else. We never drank whiskey. It was always rum and Coke for me, or sambuca for her. We were sharing a flat in Cricklewood, and she dragged me out.

She placed her hands on mine, clasping them. She only did that when something had happened. She was never one for touching. That farm girl's tongue she has on her still is better at barbs and quips. She did the same thing when Micheal died, clasped my hands, said she'd better get a drink inside me.

'He asked my ma to write.'

I noticed at the time that Aoife's hands were strangely drained of warmth.

'She didn't realise we were in London. Sure her letter went all the way to Bermuda. It found its way here.'

She was procrastinating.

'Seven months after it was posted. Would you believe that?'

I wanted her to get to the point.

'Lucky I left a forwarding address.'

Aoife sat back and sipped her drink. I knew she was thinking hard about how to proceed, because her eyes were no longer on me but on the empty ashtray. She spoke more quietly, perhaps trying to put off what she had taken me there to say.

'Ma said the father was looking very old. He must be eighty himself if he's a day.'

I realised that only one thing could have happened.

'Your mother passed away.'

It was little surprise to me that Niamh Murtagh died alone in the cottage, isolated and detached. But in Duagh it came as a surprise that she had died at all. Aoife recounted the content of her mother's letter. No one had known Niamh was ill, not even Father Hanlon, and to think she was cleaning his house right to the very end. She was made of stone.

'She did not breathe a word, the father said. She bore her pain without bothering anyone like the good woman that she was.'

I knew Aoife did not believe this. She hated my mother from childhood and the feeling was mutual. Our playtime was spent in her home, not mine, a dungeon she felt it her duty to rescue me from. But I understood those small untruths she told to blunt the edge. Kind lies, tokens of friendship.

There was more. I sat there listening thoughtfully. Aoife was in full flood. The sheer embarrassment of being a bringer of bad news when hers was always good had got the better of her. She delved further into the contents of the letter from her mother, drank more for courage, set up a denouement.

And I realised then that the complex saga of the letter's diversion by way of Bermuda was not of little consequence, and that alongside her embarrassment, Aoife somehow felt guilty.

'She's long buried now, Eileen. There's no funeral to be going to.'

It was a fitting end to a tortuous story and, I thought, appropriate. My mother was alone in death as in life. If I had been able to cry, I may have done so. But I did not. There was no weeping in the Murtagh household. It was a lesson my mother taught me. It was neither sadness nor guilt that I felt, but resignation. It was always going to be that way.

We drank more and, for the sake of Aoife, shared memories of the woman whom we both despised.

But I was haunted. The regret I felt was not for having misunderstood, because that was not true. It was for not having tried to understand.

We left the pub and returned to the flat. I lay in bed and could not fail to watch the door. Lights of cars climbing Shoot-Up Hill swept across the ceiling.

I had to decide what to do with the cottage. I wrote to Father Hanlon to thank him for his trouble. I contacted an estate agent

in Tralee and told them to clear it and sell the plot.
    '*I will never go back*,' I whispered.

9

I'm studying, trying to answer questions from an old exam paper. I want to do this. I want to pass my GCSE. I'm working as hard as I can, even though I'm stupid. I'm doing it for Eileen. She says I can do this. Maybe she's right. Just scrape through.

I'm sitting on the sofa in the front room, and the door is closed. There are noises outside on the estate, and it feels familiar. It's better here. I will not go back to my bedroom.

There is a cautious knock on the door, and I'm irritated but also surprised. I wait to listen that I have heard right. There is another knock. It can only be Stella.

You in there?

Her voice is not a sharp implement poised to stab, but I brace for something deadly anyway.

Course.

The knocking continues, insistent. Why is she knocking at all? Normally she just barges in. There is no lock on this door. I ignore her. She wants a drink or fags or chips. It's an interruption. I've got work to do.

Open the door Molly.

Stella's request is a surprise. None of the normal *'useless cow'* or *'bleedin bitch'*. Even her throat doesn't sound croaky.

I'm studying. I got an exam. I ain't got time to go to the shop.

Don't want nothing from the shop.

I'm frustrated. I put my pen down. I look through the window at the darkness outside and wonder how late it is. Roundwell is better at night. It's when the inhabitants can dream.

What do you want then?

Just let me in.

She's not swearing or cursing. I'm confused. She wants me to open the door. To let her in even though it's not locked. I push myself up and straighten my back. It's stiff and aches. I open the door. Now Stella is surprised. She steps back. Her hair is wet.

What?

Thought you wasn't going to open.

It ain't locked. I told you I can't go to the shop, I'm doing homework.

Don't want nothing from the shop.

Well what?

Stella is clutching something in her hand. She holds out her fist and opens it. It's a clump of her hair, large enough to be a small animal.

This come out. My hair. I was in the bath.

I examine her face. She's frightened. I can tell from the wide eyes and slightly open mouth awaiting an explanation from someone smarter. I can also tell because I have seen this before. Once. After Stan belted her. She sobered up just long enough for a gulp of fear, then went back to being drunk again.

So?

Well that ain't normal, is it?

You bleedin bleach it all the time, don't you. Anyone knows you can't bleach your hair all the time. Course it's going to fall out.

I din't know that. No one ever told me that.

Says so on the packet, don't it.

You know I can't read no bleedin packet.

I shrug, but in that moment I can't escape her woeful expression. She is manipulative. She knows I'll help her. But she is also frightened.

Listen, you can't keep bleedin bleaching it.

Stella starts crying. She brings her hands to her face and I watch as the clump of hair sticks to the tears rolling down her cheek. She's shaking. It's pathetic, but I feel something strange that I've never felt. I feel sorry for her. Stan has gone, Rob has gone, I ain't here, now her hair is falling out.

I reach out for her shoulder and touch it. It feels surprisingly soft. I can't recall ever touching it. She seems older. I notice wrinkles around her neck that I've never seen before.

Do you want me to do your hair?

She nods between her sobs.

Needs conditioner. You got any?

Stella nods again, then sniffs a liquid breath.

But what about your 'omework?

I shake my head. It'll have to wait.

Go to the bathroom.

She does what she is told with childlike obedience. I know she wants a drink, but she's broke and Asif has banned her from the shop.

I take something from my bag and climb the stairs. She's sitting on the toilet seat in the bathroom, dabbing her eyes. Eyeliner has blackened in rings all around them and she looks like she's been thumped by Stan again, or is a *pan-der* in a place called *Fee-at*. I brush her hair out gently. I pass her a leaflet Eileen gave me. If Stella does not stop boozing, she will croak.

Look at that.

I can't read it.

Lucky someone in this house bleedin can then, ain't it?

10

It colours her like a stain. It pushes her to the very edge of the framework in which other people live. It forces her to keep her balance on that slippery slope that is her life. Above all, it makes travelling to Whitstable difficult. Stella is unable to read the signs.

This is like the old days. At the coach station she has to get by simply by asking questions, lots of them, the stench of brandy on her breath making this a precarious exercise. People snap at her like dogs because the smell triggers rage in them. Her wild eyes and honking seal sounds want more from them than just directions.

She finds herself travelling the right way. To make sure she does not get lost she asks an old man sitting beside her five times whether she is on the coach to Canterbury.

It is late when she arrives and she has missed the last bus to Whitstable. She sleeps on a chair at the depot and no one dares to bother her. She cadges a cup of coffee in the morning from the cleaners.

Whitstable is small enough to remember. She finds the caravan site where Stan always stayed. The site manager knows him and recognises her from long ago. He fancied her then, but does not any more. Stan has been there, but he has not seen him for a while. He opens Stan's caravan and lets her wait inside.

Something happens in that solitude. As she sits there alone, Stella feels strangely calm. Complete. Unbroken. The soothing, enclosed silence once the door shuts cleanses her. The absence of things fills her with relief. She is tired, broke, hungry and desperate for a drink. But she feels better than she has for some time.

She waits. Stan does not return. The following day, she leaves. She steals a banana from a market stall, then takes the coach back to London.

Molly has not missed her. She had not known Stella was

gone. But the place looks different, as if Stella has returned to an alternative reality. Everything is as it was before, but nothing is the same.

Stella finds a few cigarettes in an old packet and sits in the kitchen smoking quietly. She hears Mrs Nally returning from her shopping and feels the vibration of the door shutting. The dog barks for food.

She trudges upstairs and lies down on her bed. She falls asleep, but now she is sleeping in a caravan.

Stella dreams of Liam. He pulls himself from the water with a triumphant smile.

'It weren't your fault. It was freezing.'

11

Eileen has been having flashbacks. Unexpected cues transport her.

As she passes a market stall in Portobello and smells incense, she finds herself in the priest's house beside St Bridget's, waiting nervously in the hall with the other children. Father Hanlon is going to talk to them in his front room before their confirmation because the roof of the church is leaking and they cannot use it.

The house smells of incense and candle wax. Her mother is there, cleaning. It is the first and will be the only time Eileen has ever seen her work. The woman dusts a bookcase and removes each volume to wipe it.

Eileen watches as she waits. The priest is on the telephone in his study. The bookcase contains a Virtue and Company full set of *Lives of the Saints*. Eileen can see this printed clearly in beautiful gold lettering on the spines. They contain coloured illustrations, and she knows this because all the children have looked through them before to help choose the names of the saints they wish to take at their confirmation.

She watches as her mother slides out each book carefully, but is surprised she does not flick through to look at the pictures. This is her favourite book.

Eileen is in the school canteen on lunch duty, the clatter of hungry children echoing. She smells boiled cabbage, and then finds herself back in the kitchen of the cottage where she grew up. Her mother stands rigid over a pot hanging from the crane. She watches it cook as if that were required.

This is how Eileen remembers her, only ever in the kitchen, washing laundry in the scullery, scraping it on a washboard, feeding it through the mangle in the yard. Never in the field with Finbar.

It is disconcerting, because her mother was from farming folk. That is why she married him. A farmer needs a wife. But then again, it is not a farm. It is a glorified vegetable patch with a pig fed scraps and whatever falls from an apple tree.

Eileen is in the pub with the other teachers listening to the chink of glasses and soft patter of conversation, then suddenly she finds herself outside O'Brady's looking through the window, standing on tiptoes to see her father inside. He throws on his cap as he leaves and strolls with her back to the cottage, whispering conspiratorially. He hopes the cigarette smoke in his jacket will mask the odour of porter.

'Don't tell your mother, now.'

She sees that burning anger in her mother's eyes when she smells his breath. The woman marches to the hall for her coat and takes from it her Pioneer temperance pin. She stabs it at her blouse to mock the poor man, and sits there wringing her hands as she bubbles, rubbing her wrists as if in pain. She turns the conversation to the Sacred Heart, and stares at her daughter across the table.

Eileen sees dismay in her father's face. She wants to stand and hug his neck.

These memories provide only fragments of a story.

12

Stella has gone to sleep. Good riddance. But the image of her face lingers. I have never seen her like that. Vulnerable.

I curl over my paper and start to write under the light in the front room. Eileen bought me a bulb. I am answering another question about *An Inspector Calls*. I write.

'Arthur is really posh and rich ...'

I look at my book. I have to check something. I flick through the pages. A dog barks outside. I know I have overlooked Eric. He's only a character in a book, but I'm resisting.

'Eric is the son. Sheila's brother. He's kind of there, but not, at the same time. Like, missing.'

I ask myself whether I'm writing about Eric at all. I'm alone here and describing what is in an old book, but I feel discomfort and an urge to change the subject. It's as if I'm being monitored by something far more powerful than me.

I look around the room to check that I'm alone. I know it's irrational, but I sense I'm being observed. It was how I felt at school, that they were inside my head, knew exactly what I was thinking.

I snap shut my copy of *An Inspector Calls* and put down my pen. I wait for the dog outside to bark again, but there is only silence.

Then I hear Eileen. She's giving me permission to write what I think. To explore my every thought. She says I am not useless.

She has this way. An ability to understand me. I will do this for her. I pick up the pen.

'Eric's an alcoholic. He drinks too much and can't stop. It sort of makes him a bit stupid, really, but his family ignore him because they don't really want to deal with it.'

It doesn't matter what I write. No one will ever know what I

think. They're not watching me. I understand that now.
   'Alcoholics make life awkward for everyone.'

13

Stella's mother wants to thrash her. Hit her with the strap, like the auld fella used to. God knows the child deserves it. She wants to leave red, burning welts the shape of her palm on her little pink thighs, buttocks, cheeks. She wants to bruise her daughter, blacken her defiant big blue eyes, teach her a lesson she'll never forget, scream at her, cover her face with raging spittle, burst those eardrums that never listen to a word she says. She wants to kick and tear and drag and scratch this child, make sure she knows what she has done, and carries the scar of it forever. She wants to shake her to make her understand.

'I lost the baby ...

Instead, she locks Stella in the bedroom of the caravan, shuts out her whimpering pleas, starves the ungrateful tyke for as long as she can get away with it.

Even when they reach the next site, and the cage she has created contains nothing but exhausted despair, she does not let Stella out, leaves the latch hooked, cooks steaming pots that rattle, wallows outside in the mud of their wretched lives.

'... and it's your fault you useless sow ...

She forces herself not to look at the window of the children's room and turns her back to it, but she still wonders. She wonders whether, if she were to turn suddenly, Liam would be there, half hanging out the caravan, hiding his boyish guilt behind that little grin.

He cares little, Stella's father. He watches his wife punishing the girl, but says nothing, busy rolling dirty cash with the rest of them. His heart burst long ago. He does not intervene, put down his foot, lay down the law. Enough is not enough.

Delirious from thirst Stella is when her mother finally pulls back the latch. Skin and bones beneath the bed, grieving in her own childish way, because that is all she can do in her imprisonment. The girl cannot make head nor tail of it all.

'... I even had a name ...

Her mother decides that guilt is what her daughter needs, and so force feeds her plenty thereafter. Guilt for breakfast, dinner, and tea. Silence for her pudding. But little for her mouth. Even the dogs turn their backs to make her feel unwanted.

Stella dreams of him in that little bedroom, her Liam, and asks him to intercede. She lies beneath the blanket imagining he is there, and she is brushing the coarse fibres of his hair with her fingers. She sobs dryly because there's nothing left with which to weep. Her mother sobs outside.

'... I was going to call her Molly.'

Stella's brother whispers kindly that it's not her fault, but he cannot intercede. He's dead and gone and rotting in the soil.

Stella grieves with such force she almost joins him, and wonders what would have been if they had stayed at the school with the slide and the footie field. And if she'd had a baby sister.

14

I have started to put things in boxes. I am sorting out what to take to Ireland. It is very little. The rest will go to the charity shop. I have gone over all the furniture. Most of it is utilitarian and can be passed on. I will take my bed and my reclining armchair.

I bring down the contents of my small attic and spread it out in the living room. Papers, mostly, old bank statements, clutter, correspondence, school reports, pointless photographs. The residue of a lifetime. Most of what I find goes into black plastic sacks. It is surprisingly easy. I wonder why I kept it in the first place.

There is nothing from my childhood. We did not have a camera. I have no photograph of the cottage. My father. My mother.

I come across a letter. Father Hanlon understood. He said so before he died. I shall not keep it, but read it one last time.

'Her own mother died in childbirth.'

My heart misses a beat as I see Niamh there, standing in the kitchen looking out. I lack any desire to understand our differences or how I might help her solve the riddle of her unhappiness. I swing on to my bicycle under the stern gaze of this loveless shell, arms crossed, the picture of a farmer's wife. Small but indomitable. Omnipotent.

'Her father was a tyrant for the drink. Died before you were born.'

I think about the priest. He would know all about drink, after all. He buried the publican O'Brady for free, so large was the chit he owed him, and they were all square when the pub landlord's feckless son succeeded him. That boy was more a poet than a publican. There was a special place in my mother's heart for her hatred of the dishevelled, red-haired slacker forever peering at the sky.

'She loved God, if not those around her.'

Niamh throws a bunch of carrots to me across the kitchen table. They land with a dull thud, like corpses. She storms into the other room. I hear the door slam shut, and in despair pick up the carrots and dip them in the enamel bucket. The water is so cold it burns. I shake my hands to ease the pain. I sit and begin to chop. The mechanical motion dulls my senses. I put the carrots to boil, then prepare potatoes as well to put her in good humour.

'Her family was the church.'

It is dark now, and I hear her shuffling downstairs. I am sitting on my bed. She has locked me in my room. I light a candle. When I look out the window all I see is my own reflection, shuddering in the candlelight. My face shifts uneasily against the glass as if trying to escape me.

Father Hanlon made it worse. After mass, in full view, he told O'Brady to take a housekeeper. It was the only time I ever saw her blush.

'But I know you suffered, child.'

When I was out of sorts, under the weight of her unbending strictures, I committed an act of spite. In my mind I put her in a pinafore and on her knees, scrubbing the wooden planks in the public bar of O'Brady's as his useless heir watched while dreaming idly of Raglan Road.

'Forgive her, Eileen.'

15

M y brain. Sure, I feel it moving. A lifeless lump it is, a tumour. It slides inside my head, down into my neck, pushing past my Adam's apple. I feel it in my throat and cannot speak, cannot say a word.

It's left behind a hole, and this fills up with the sound of Stella screeching slurs at me. I hear my name, *'Stan'*, but I don't know what she's talking about because the echoes bounce around my skull, crashing into each other with such angry force their meaning is smashed to smithereens. I don't understand. Sure, why would I?

I'm in the hallway in Roundwell like I was that night, but at the same time I'm not. It's as if I've been cut with scissors from a family photograph that we do not have and there is just an empty space. There is the front door, concrete-coloured light struggling through the frosted glass, the hall bare with its matted carpet, a grubbed space on the wallpaper where a picture might once have hung.

My brain is passing from my throat along my shoulder. I watch the bump beneath my skin as it skates towards my arm. How is this possible? To have a brain that moves?

I pick among Stella's broken sounds with my brittle, chipped fingernails, the tar still beneath them, left over from a job. Nothing is complete. Everything is wrecked. I dig through the half-words and snapped and cracking curses for something I can recognise.

I find a word.

'... *you* ...

but to make use of this I need another, so I search for something else bombarding my echo chamber, anything less damaged,

'... *you're* ...

She's angry and I wish I knew why. This is how I feel all the time, trying to understand why Stella is angry. In the hallway, in the kitchen, in the bathroom, in the bedroom. It's a moment on a loop, it's happened so many times, and all I ever see is fury. Even her blonde hair turns red.

I want to speak, to ask what have I done, to put it right, say sorry, but my lips are sealed. I never speak. Sure, aren't I the silent dog that sniffs around the caravan sites, meek, starved, abused? She slaps me when she chooses. But then again, sometimes she throws a bone.

My brain turns now into my upper arm.

I feel it pressing against the muscle, which I know is strong for all the blackstuff it has spread. The bulge crawls beneath my flesh like gel and I stand and watch, captivated. Stella is dizzy. Her bitten words leap inside the vacuum of my head and become clearer as her voice lowers, ready for the climax.

'... *look ... at ... me ... you ... bleedin ...*

My brain plops over the bones in my elbow with a wobble and slithers down my forearm towards my hand and I feel it pulsing, gorged with blood, inflating,

'... *useless ... lucky ... I've ...*

My fingers tingle as it fills them like a glove and then I sense their clawing touch. Half-fingers, half-brain, where my mind resides. I hear one last string of sounds inside my head, clearer now, her voice slowing as does time itself around me,

'... *got ... Rob ...* '

And as my hand clenches into a fist I discover, at last, that my brain has a purpose.

16

'*I*'*m coming too.*'
I take off my dress and stand there in the cold in just my knickers. I'm no chicken. I throw it on top of Liam's clothes, draped across the sign, and they hang there together. He grins that grin at me and holds out his hand. I take it and he leads me to the edge of the outcrop. He positions his feet carefully, and watches me as I copy him. He knows everything, so this must be important.

'*Ready?*

He is so brave my brother, I want to be as brave as he is, do what he does. I want to be loved like he is.

'*Ready.*'

I nod and smile as courageously as I can, although even in a dream I'm frightened because the outcrop of the quarry is high and the water far below. I glimpse at the sky just before he starts to count, and notice that it has turned to night. An unearthly light picks us out from the darkness.

'*One ...*

Liam again looks at me for reassurance. It melts my heart like white chocolate, that smile.

'*Two ...*

I focus and see the ripples on the surface even though it is now night. Is that moonlight?

'*Tree!*'

He jumps and I feel him tug my hand and pull me with him. Together we are somersaulting through the air, spinning in motion that is even purer than the roundabout in the playground, arms and feet thrown out by spiralling force. I want to stay like this forever, levitating, neither on the ground nor in the water, nowhere near reality. I see Liam smiling too and realise that he wants this to be so as well. We are in unison, the bond unbreakable, refugees from a land into which we were never born.

Then we hit the surface.

It is so ice cold it squeezes the air from my lungs. I close my eyes and sink, aware of bubbles around me, tickling my skin, filling my ears. I thrash against the drag of the liquid, waiting for it to stabilise. I know I should surface and wait, but I cannot. I open my eyes and search for Liam, but I am alone. I can move neither up nor down, sink nor swim. I am suspended. All is silent.

Suddenly there's movement. Someone is kicking, and in the distance Liam fights against a current. His eyes are wide and he is no longer grinning and he signals with his hand and shouts, and I hear his voice, muffled by the freezing water. He is dying slowly.

'Too cold ... I am drown-ded, Stella ...

He points furiously and waves his arms with panicked urgency. He shouts and shouts. He disappears from view.

I turn away and try to swim but the water is no longer clear but brown and tastes of brandy and I like it too much to want to leave so I ignore the distant echo.

'... save yourself.'

I open my mouth and swallow. The liquid enters my throat and lungs and stomach, and for a moment I am content. I am swimming in a reservoir of drink. I like the taste too much to stop. I drink and drink. Everything seems clearer.

But now I cannot breathe. I feel my limbs becoming limp. I begin to sink. I am drowning too. The light is fading.

I wake up, dumbfounded, and realise that I am dreaming. A dream that is not a drunken dream is filled with the horror of potential. A nightmare that could have happened.

I understand what this means, for now I am sober.

17

I waved when Aoife passed through the departure gate. I fought back a tear. She mouthed at me from the other side, pointing with her free hand. I realised what she was saying.

'You're next Eileen!'

It was not as if she was going far, or as if she hadn't been back already. She was returning to Ireland. She had been back many times by herself, to see her parents, sister, brother, nieces, nephews. But this time she was going back for good. I would see her soon enough, but it was a watershed.

We had been together a lifetime, since long before she joined me in Liverpool. We grew up together, travelled together, lived together, laughed and wept together. She was the sister I never had, loyally following me into teaching, Liverpool, Bermuda, and London. Holidays in France and Spain. Trips to the sea and the country. Pubs and clubs and restaurants, endless walks in rolling landscapes. This would be the first time we had been separated since our teenage years.

But her health has been failing and she still has a family. The generation that flocked to England for a future is going home. It was her time.

Aoife disappeared into the security hall and I turned and walked to the car park. Her embrace lingered. It was like none I have experienced. We looked at each other and knew that time was expiring. The future was no longer open. We were no longer escaping the constraints of a rural childhood ever since skipping free all those years ago.

I also knew that it would not be long before I join her. I will stay with her until I find myself a home. We are so used to each other it will come naturally.

I am retired, but continue working only at the request of Bernadette Kavanagh. She was desperate. But my mind is made up.

I have set a date to leave. I have visited an estate agent and they have taken details of the house. I have contacted a removal company. Boxes are piling up in the living room and the furniture has been disappearing in the weeks leading up to the GCSEs.

18

N ight is when Stan does his thinking. The lack of light leaves space for him to fill, a scoured road waiting for tar. It makes it easier to think. He calibrates the darkness of his mind, and sets to it.

He has never been a heavy sleeper, his ears attuned since childhood to faint sounds in the empty distance of the countryside. They keep him on the edge of slumber.

So he thinks, although this is never easy. It comes to him in the endless, sleepless night. Driveways. He starts with the problem as he sees it. The problem is Whitstable. It seems too small, at least compared to other places. Canterbury, that is. There are not enough driveways. That is why he is always short of work.

This is not a profound thought, but it is for Stan. Instinct tells him he needs to go somewhere with lots of houses and cars. It would mean buckling down, staying in one place, gritting his teeth. It is not as if he does not know how to grit his teeth. He put up with Stella, didn't he? He can take the rough with the smooth, even if there is a lot more rough than smooth. Fortunately, Stan is low maintenance. He gets by on a shoestring.

Stan looks through the window at the stars. It is a clear night, and his head is clear as well. It is as if the sky over Whitstable is a barometer for what is going on in his mind. Mostly cloudy, sometimes stormy, always unpredictable, occasionally clear.

All he has to do is figure out where to go. Anxious to hold on to this thought, not forget it instantly, he begins to list places. He gets no farther than Canterbury. It is big. There are lots of houses. It is near Whitstable. And there would be bin work. Stan knows this because he has seen the garbage teams collecting just like they do on Roundwell.

He has never touted for work. Others do the touting, he does the grafting. Entire tar families do driveways, farmers' lanes, cattle yards, and he works for them when there is work to be done. He does not just lay asphalt, mind. He has other strings to his bow. He does concrete and paving. The Callaghans left him to do the concrete for a cattle shed and Frankie gave him an extra fifty quid because it was a good job.

Frankie has a skill for touting. He goes up to a door and rings the bell and just speaks. It spills out. He makes it look easy. A kind of poetry. Mind you, Frankie could talk the tide into handing over cash. It was something Stan has never dreamed of doing. Words just do not come. He is tongue tied. He'd get it wrong, mess it up, he knows he would.

It is at moments like these that Stan could have despaired, but he does not see his limitations as a question of inadequacy. He cannot imagine himself as someone else, an improved version. He knows what he can do, just like he knows what Frankie can do. And Stan cannot tout.

Stan stares out of the caravan until dawn trying to figure out the depths of this dilemma. By the time the sun is rising, his mind has exhausted his body. He goes to sleep. There is no work for him that day.

*

The students stand in small groups outside the hall, fidgeting, shuffling their feet. They are trying to stay calm, appear in control. Desperation clutches at the air with the thinnest of hope. There is the hum of nervous chatter. They anticipate what is coming and the challenge they now face.

Tutors mill about, impatient. They wait for the doors to open so that they can shepherd their charges in. It is the very end of the job that they have to do, and now it is up to the children themselves to make of it what they can. Inside, through the windows, invigilators place examination papers on desks with quiet efficiency. It could be any school.

Bridie stands with others from her group, ready to enter.

They are trying to be brave, propping each other up, because they know that this is something they must face. But they are dying inside. She is smarter than ever, having made an effort for this special day, her clothing a way to control her fear.

Eileen asks Bridie how she feels, then reassures her. She is grateful to this lippy girl who was excluded for her cheek and never takes a teacher's comment lying down.

Have you seen Molly?

Bridie shakes her head.

Eileen checks her watch and trembles unexpectedly. A spasm jolts her into realising she has not considered a possibility. Would the refusenik in Molly return at the moment of truth?

Then Eileen is torn by conflicting thoughts. Has she handled this correctly? Has she been sufficiently on top of Molly's feelings? Is there something she has overlooked?

She reflects on the dark presence that hangs over the girl, the shadow of Stella, a tectonic deformation, a dangerous, jagged landscape impossible to traverse.

Eileen concludes that she should have arranged to pick Molly up in the car. She should have insisted. It is too late now.

The doors of the hall open and the students start to enter. They weave in and out of the rows finding their candidate numbers, sitting on cold seats, noticing the large, ominous clock draped on an easel at the front. Anxiety is palpable, a clawing atmosphere with a dense presence. Whispered chatter is of good luck and reassurance.

Eileen checks her watch again. There are fifteen minutes to go before the exam starts. She walks into the secretary's office. She can see the entrance of the Mudlark centre from there. She picks up the telephone.

*

Do us a favour ...

The driver does not have time for this. He cannot just *'drop her off at the corner'* unless she pays her fare. He has more important things to worry about. The bus is holding up the traffic, and this dishevelled blonde circus act with a sheepskin coat over her nightdress is holding up the other passengers.

Stella looks down the aisle at Molly, who has gone ahead, embarrassed by her mother, expecting trouble. She is sitting opposite the door pretending that Stella is nothing to do with her.

Defeated, the driver jabs his thumb to the interior of the bus. *Just get on.*

Stella walks along the aisle and throws herself on the seat. Molly turns away from her and stares coldly out the window.

Din't have to come.

Stella makes herself comfortable and looks around at the other passengers.

Only want to be dropped off ... just a favour ...

The hydraulic doors of the bus exhale and close. The vehicle pulls out with a jerk. Stella relaxes, oblivious to the stress she is causing.

... no big deal ...

She begins to fumble in the pockets of her sheepskin and brings out a packet of cigarettes. She withdraws one, watched suspiciously by an old man sitting opposite. His eyes flicker to a '*No Smoking*' sign on the window right beside them. She sees him.

Molly tenses, steeling herself for trouble. Stella must feel her body go stiff, because she conceals her hand, then speaks above the noise of the bus for the man to hear.

Ain't going to smoke it. Just need to hold it.

The bus jolts and Molly grasps a rail to steady herself.

Eileen had offered to pick her up and take her to the centre, but she had said no. She was hoping the bus journey would calm her nerves. Now she wished she had said yes.

Molly was at the front door of the house when Stella, still in her nightdress, announced she was going with her. It was an unexpected burden when she least needed it. Her mother pulled on her sheepskin and waddled after her across the estate telling her to wait up, not knowing where she was going or how to get there. Molly led and she followed.

They sit in silence on the bus, side by side. Stella senses her daughter's anger.

Just felt it might help ...

Molly shuts her eyes, and tries to blank out her voice,

... someone being with you ...

but the image of Stella in the bathroom returns and she is weeping at her falling hair,

... this being a big day and all ...

holding up a clump for Molly to see,

... I'm your mother, after all.

*

Stan stands at the gate and surveys a pitted moonscape. Potholes in the decaying concrete are still blotted with puddles from the previous day's rain. Ageing cement and gravel clots in jagged clumps that have broken away in scattered chaos. Pebbles from the aggregate litter the surface, kicked by everyone making their way to and from the front door. A lip of uneven pavers threatens to trip those who dare to cross them.

This house needs a new driveway.

He examines it. The house is scruffy, but it is not sad. The windows have been replaced with new double glazing. On the porch are potted plants that do not wilt. The front door has been painted.

His mind races. All night he played out a conversation with the man who would open this door. Even in his mind, the words came out jumbled. A man who opened the door in his imagination bore a strong resemblance to Frankie. He laughed at Stan then slammed it in his face.

'Bogger off tievin poikey.'

So Stan practised, hard, in front of the cracked mirror so much that it hurt his head. He is not used to talking.

'D'yous want your drive doin? D'yous want a new drive,

sure now? D'yous need a drive? I see yous need a new drive. Your drive is broken. Your drive needs fixin. That drive of yours, sure it's old. Do you not need a new drive now? Should I be doin your drive for yous? See sor, I noticed your drive is in need of doin. See sor, I was passin and ...'

He clenches his fists with frustration and voices the possibilities again. He tries to order his thoughts. What is he trying to say? He hears his father. The old fellow is looking up from his pint.

'Just say what you mean, man.'

On the bus journey from Whitstable to Canterbury, Stan practises, the voices in his head crowding out everything. Something strange occurs. He remembers what happened to the little donkey in the story. Before it went to heaven. He misses his stop.

*

From the edge of my eye, I see the main doors of the centre swing open. My heart lifts. I am almost sick with relief. Molly's slight form enters. Stella is behind her.

I put down the telephone and walk out of the office to meet them. Molly is pale as a sheet. She wrings her hands. I don't think it is because of the exam. It is because of Stella.

Stella is awkward, out of place. She scans the corridor and foyer like a frightened animal. But she seems different. I do not have time to figure out why. Her hair looks different, I think. I cannot smell alcohol on her breath. I am surprised to see her. I weigh up what has just happened. Stella is showing support. This is not something I have seen before. I feel gratitude, but also apprehension. She has never done this. Molly is in uncharted territory.

I was getting a bit worried. Everything okay Molly?

The girl puts on a brave face, but is wound up like a coiled spring. Stella appears to be in a state of confusion. She is holding a cigarette, but appears to have forgotten she is doing so. Molly reminds her.

Put your bleedin fag away.

Stella fumbles with the packet.

So this is your college is it?

Molly points to a room beside the hall.

That's my class there.

I am aware that time is moving on. I press gently.

I'll show Stella when you get settled in. Let's get you to your desk.

I lead them to the hall. Molly hesitates at the doorway. Stella pushes her head inside to see the other young people lined up, their fear something she can smell. She tries to read Molly, but it is difficult. Yet there in the child's face is something she recognises. Stella opens her arms, and her own instinct takes her by surprise.

The hug is as clumsy as the lid of a pan. I know at once this is not something that happens often, if it has ever happened at all. I also know that I am witnessing a miracle.

As she embraces Molly, Stella catches my eye. She stretches an uneasy smile. I decide that it is genuine.

She'll be all right, won't she Eileen?

Yes, she will.

Molly turns to face the hall. I put my hand on her shoulder and look into her eyes. The desperation they contain is so deep I begin to understand. At any moment the refusenik within her could turn and run and not stop until she finds herself in her bedroom. But this Molly Path does not run. I try to reassure her.

Write what you feel.

Her face is taut and she glances at the floor, but she wants to be confident. Bridie is in her seat and looks back at her friend then beckons her over. Molly takes a last look at her mother, then goes to her place. The doors of the hall close.

Stella does not know what to do with her hands. Her fingers stretch and click. She is distracted, unaware of her surroundings, and again takes out a cigarette. For a woman with a sharp tongue, for once she is lost for words.

I show her the classroom where I taught Molly's group. It

appears to hold special significance. Her eyes are wide in wonder. She is imprinting what she sees.

I accompany her to the exit. She takes me by surprise.

Thank you.

Then she extends her arms and hugs me also, in that awkward pan-lid way. I watch her walk across the playground to the gate.

I do not know why, but I am proud of her.

*

Stan reaches the house that he has chosen. His heart pounds louder than a wacker plate. He knows he cannot go back. It is one of those moments in life, like birth or death. He steps through the gate and walks down the drive, examining the contours and gradient of the ground.

He pictures a new drive with a straight edge by the small wall and a gentle curve abutting the lawn. He can see it clearly. In asphalt, in patterned concrete, in paving slabs, in cobbles, even in silver paving blocks. He can imagine that driveway in the future, with a car rolling smoothly on it, the house smiling down as if it were its birthday. He wants to fix it, make it new again, give the people who live here something special.

He stands before the door, a portal, frozen, petrified of what lies within. He holds his finger an inch from the doorbell. It hovers and his attention is drawn to the dirt beneath his chipped nails.

Then it opens. He looks at his finger in surprise because he has not yet pressed the button.

A woman stands there with a little girl clamped to her hip. Her hair is tousled and she is pale, her skin nearly grey, worn out, her complexion a long domestic sigh. The child's blonde ringlets glow like gold.

The woman sees Stan as if she knows him and her eyes widen. He grows fearful. She is either too familiar, or making an accusation. He has done nothing wrong. He does not work with Frankie any more.

She gestures with her chin at the driveway, unable to point with her hands.

I know why you're here. I saw you looking. I know what you're going to say, and you're right. Give me a price, and I'll talk to my husband.

*

Bernadette Kavanagh looks at me from above her reading glasses with an intensity that confirms it will be the last time she ever sees me. It is known but not said. We have worked together on and off for years. I respect her, and I know the feeling is mutual.

She stands beside the only space upon a cabinet that is not piled with folders where there is a tray with a bottle of sherry and two glasses. The piles are precarious and I fear they will topple, submerging this small, rotund woman. All I would see would be her swollen ankles sticking out from under an avalanche. In all the years I have been at the Mudlark, those piles have never gone down.

She hands me a glass and toasts my imminent departure.

Slainte!

I repay the compliment.

We down our drinks, and I notice she pours herself another. She is overweight and I worry about her. I can hear her wheezing faintly as she manoeuvres herself into her chair. It is not just the stress of the job, the constant need to justify the centre's existence and fight its corner, it is also that she has not looked after herself. She is a matriarch who has always put her family first: pupils, parents, teachers. The damage this has done is visible in her stooped gait, the folds of fat on her neck, the ruddy, venous cheeks, the sheen of perspiration.

Sunlight streams through the large bay window that looks out upon the school field. I have always liked this room. As I watch her, I reflect on the ease with which she has slipped into and out of the lives of the troubled children passing through. She has navigated the complex twists and turns of their countless problems in a search for their promised land like a captain at sea.

She says she is struggling to recall how many pupils I have tutored over the years.

You know, I always gave you the toughest of the bunch?

It is true. We laugh.

It looks like you got Molly to the finishing line.

I look across the field and smile. Bernadette quizzes me with her expression. I tell the truth.

It turns out we had something in common.

As I leave, she stands by the main door and waves. I fight back a tear as I walk from the centre for the last time. It is not like a Murtagh to cry, but this is the end of a long story that has defined me. Now it is over.

*

Stella sits in front of the large mirror. She examines her face, eyes burning blue, well-defined cheekbones, the clear line of her lips. The wrinkles seem less upsetting now. There is a seriousness that she had been lacking.

The hairdresser sweeps a towel across her shoulders then pulls a nylon wrap around her neck and presses the Velcro seal together at the back. She examines Stella's hair and can see long roots showing through. The new growth has some bounce, but the old, blonde ends are flaky, dry, and formless. Like the cut stubble in a field.

They both examine the face and hair in the mirror, their eyes meeting. The hairdresser presses her comb into Stella's scalp and pulls gently, working out the hair with her skilled fingers, her nails displaying embedded diamonds.

We bleaching it again?

Stella looks at the bottles of hair treatment arranged in rows along the shelf. A chemical army. She tries to recall the first time she bleached her hair. Her mother had kicked her out. She was hiding behind it.

She reaches up and fingers the hair away from the scalp so that the roots are clearly visible. It is weak and soft, but does not come away in her hand. She shakes her head.

No.

The hairdresser is content. This is a discussion she is accustomed to. It is the right decision.

My girl told me not to.

Sensible.

The hairdresser starts to comb out Stella's hair ready for a wash.

So what's your daughter up to?

Stella feels a weightlessness. It pushes her from below. She is rising. It is something she has not felt before.

Just got her GCSE.

The hairdresser is impressed. She pouts. She runs the water and tests it with her hand, then washes Stella's hair with shampoo and rinses it. She dabs it dry.

So I'm just cutting it am I? Same but layered?

Stella examines her head in the mirror, her expression stern and uncompromising.

Shorter, reckon. Cut those ends off. Change of image.

The hairdresser gets to work, her fingers busy snipping away the split ends. Stella continues.

She wants to get a job.

The face in the mirror nods acknowledgment.

So how do you become a stylist?

The woman does not look up from her work, and speaks between the clacking scissor blades.

She could go to college. Or train on the job, like I did. Find a salon what needs a trainee.

Stella listens carefully. She will report back everything she learns.

So how d'you know if they need a trainee?

I suppose they put a note in the window. That's how I got my job.

Stella watches her new self emerging. She is not displeased.

When they are finished and she pays, she glances at the window to see if there is a card there.

Don't suppose they need a trainee here?

The hairdresser says she will ask the boss.

*

Aoife is waiting at Farranfore airport. She hugs Eileen warmly. She has not been back in Ireland herself for very long, but even so their separation has been unusual.

It is still light and Eileen breathes in the cool air. It tastes as foreign as she had felt when she first set foot in England. It is a lot to take in, being back. They walk to Aoife's car.

Do you want to go straight home?

Eileen cannot stay still. She wants to remain in motion. That way she will not have to confront the momentous choice she has made.

Let's drive.

The green is striking. She had forgotten. She sits silently and takes it in, the flatlands around the airport giving way to hills. She is surprised at the traffic. It is no longer a land of short-cuts from the boreen, inquisitive heifers poking at the wire, summer shoots, limp cow parsley beside foxgloves on the verges, buttercups with tendrils.

She is gripped by a need. They stop at a florist and she buys a bouquet. They head east, to the little cemetery of Duagh. She leaves Aoife in the car and walks hesitantly past a painted Christ between crooked headstones stained with lichen.

Light rain now sweeps across the fields and a soft wind blows in her face. It conceals her tears as she steps between the graves looking at the names. She has a faint recollection of standing beside her father's many years before.

This image pulls her, and there it is, abutting the stone wall that gives on to a boggy meadow. She touches the headstone, and smiles at him. His memory lingers, as does his voice.

She turns and stands, humble now. Her mother's grave is beside his. She crouches, and puts down her flowers.

When she first tries to remember, all she can think of is cold metal that does not bend. A complex, unyielding woman who did not know how to smile and robbed her of a childhood. Motherhood was a wooden spoon, punishment and recrimination, hours spent locked in a bedroom, strong fingers gripping her wrists.

Then Eileen pictures her there, in that very place, standing at her husband's grave. Niamh Murtagh stares into an open pit. The rain is filling it already, the water sliding from the sliced clay. An old gravedigger across the way leans idle on his spade. He waits.

And Eileen sees her kneeling in a church. Alone.

Forgive me.

*

There is a rap on the front door. The bell is still not working, but Molly has become accustomed to the sound of knocking. There is only ever one visitor. It is always Eileen. But she has gone.

Stella is in the kitchen. Washing dishes. An avalanche has transformed Bowl Mountain into Paradise Valley with a lake of lemon soapsuds, and light now floods in with such enthusiasm that she has put a pot plant on the window sill. It is growing into the space of this new world that she is creating. She does not hear the knock. She is listening to a radio.

Molly is in her bedroom. She has a supply of books to read from Eileen's attic and her dressing table is now a bookshelf. She no longer covers the mirror with a cereal packet, the books conceal it for her.

She has resolved to teach her mother how to read. A good teacher can change a life.

She puts down her book and waits for Stella to open the front door. But there is another knock, so Molly slips out of her room and slides down the stairs.

She pulls the door open slowly, for she is still not used to visitors. She feels her heartbeat rising. Doors bring change.

Stan stands in front of her.

He is the same, his sweatshirt and trousers splashed with cement and smeared with tar, his spiky, cropped hair uncombed, gleaming with a greasy sheen.

He smiles as if it were yesterday, his warm grey eyes breaking like a wave across his face, his cracked lips revealing a missing tooth.

He holds a puppy. It is bemused. Its big eyes try to take in everything.

He thrusts the small creature at Molly and it yelps. She takes it in her hands. It licks her fingers like ice cream.

Acknowledgements

My thanks go first and foremost to Margaret Broderick, my great friend and the inspiration for this book, and the brilliant author Martin Godleman (*1909; Mercy; Our Days are Few; We're West Ham United*), both former teachers of students with mental health issues. Like so many professionals who work with troubled children at the sharp end of social problems, they are unsung heroes who persistently change lives for the better but whose work is often invisible. Martin generously shared his expertise and experience, and without his insights I could not have written *Molly Path*. I am also grateful to my lifelong friend and fellow writer Felicity Goodall (*The People's War; Exodus Burma; A Question of Conscience: Conscientious Objection in the Two World Wars*) whose careful reading of my manuscript and recommendations made it immeasurably better. I am immensely thankful to Ellis Delmonte of Hawkwood Books for having the courage and confidence to publish *Molly Path*. By giving unheard voices like me a chance, independent publishers such as Hawkwood play an indispensable role in the literary world, too often with little reward. Ellis publishes beautiful, timeless books, and is helped in that task by artists such as Nikki Daigneault, to whom I am very grateful for her thoughtful, creative and original work on the cover of Molly Path. Finally my thanks go to my amazing, talented wife Georgina and daughters Isabel, Nina and Caitlin for their endless support, encouragement and forbearance.

About the author

Gavin Eugene O'Toole is a freelance journalist, editor and writer. For most of his career he worked as a sub-editor on national newspapers. He has lived in Mexico and has written six non-fiction books about Latin America. He has won several writing competitions including the Listowel Writers' Week short story and humorous essay competitions, and the Ovacome competition, and has been second, a runner-up, shortlisted or highly commended in others. He is married with three daughters and lives in London. Twitter: @GOTwrites, Web: geotoole.uk